Driver

By Sebastian Vice

 URBAN PIGS PRESS

urbanpigspress.co.uk

Front cover design by Cody Sexton.

(Anxiety Driven Graphics)

ISBN: 9781068626128

For all the lost souls wandering in the dark,

Broken and bruised,

Fucked up and strung out,

May you find your path someway,

And in the process,

Stumble upon peace someday.

Part One: Rick

Chapter 1

Midnight wind ripped through my clothes as I stumbled through the graveyard, my soul tattooed with the blood of degenerates, my hands still shaking with Henry's. Did turning his face into hamburger seal my fate, or was it sealed before conception?

Maria's gravestone would be littered with last week's flowers, and todays are half wilted. The bottle of Johnnie Walker shook as my hand struggled drinking. Limping along, my sciatica wouldn't be a problem much longer. Looking up at the sky, Elizabeth would be proud. That someone like me took time to ponder the vastness of it all, wondering which stars had died millions of years ago?

A girl like her should be ok. Well, as ok as any of us. I wish I'd be around to see her chase dreams. And maybe, just maybe, she would overcome her birth gamble. If anyone could, it would be her.

Maria used to tell me the hard times reveal who a person is. She said we leave so much from pain and suffering, but so little from comfort. What did my road of misery teach me? There's a small tombstone of a child;

Edward Smith

October 27th, 1943 – September 1st, 1948.

No caption. How did he die? Reaching *my* end, this boy died at the right age. Before the world damaged him. Isn't that a beautiful thing? To die as innocently as a child? With so few memories to haunt you before the reaper steals you.

I leaned against the cold quartz and tied off my left arm. A crow settled on a twisted tree and squawked. My head, full of broken bottles, rested on the tomb- stone, and I took another swing to numb the pain. What's worse, feeling numb, or feeling too much pain? They say feeling something, anything, is better than feeling nothing. That never seemed right.

The plot next to hers remained empty, earmarked for me. Jesus Christ, how things have a way of turning out. I do hope Elizabeth is ok. If she is, maybe my life would mean something.

"If you're out there, Maria, I tried, I really did." The air burned my lungs, and pictures of Maria's face banged around my skull, juxtaposed to spheres of violence: White dresses and long kisses, then blood- soaked hands. Maria's smile and warm touch, then the terror in the eyes of men I'd killed. Her angelic perfume, then gunpowder that lingered in the air. She'd always been a candle among nightmares, who moved with the grace of a broken angel, even if her presence was now blood smeared over a cracked mirror. If only you could see yourself as I see you, she used to say. My vein fattened, and my leg felt better after another swig.

"I could'a been hell'va racecar driver, ya?" The booze couldn't prevent tears flowing like disjointed memories washed down the gutter. She'd cleaned me up over two decades ago, yet here I am, breaking a promise, filling a syringe with my old dose. "The way I see it, my time's pretty well passed. I reckon it passed a long time ago, and I was too stupid to realize it." More tears. "I reckon it passed when you did."

No more race cars.

No more pretty girls with the blue ribbons at finish lines.

No more beautiful gasoline.

No more songful engines ringing in my ears.

Just a soul like bone scraped over concrete.

All that remained were low-rent pimps too cheap to supply condoms, and chandelier people, the type who swirled fancy wines and sucked expensive cigars at lavish dinner parties. The upper-class degenerates who popped barbiturates while ranting about the scourge of marijuana. You know the type, the kind of people who worried about street crime, while manipulating the stock market. And the blue-collar intellectual pimps howling about late-stage capitalism while taking the lion's share of their prostitutes' earnings. Like a preacher, they'd lambast the right-wing rhetoric of women's equality, reproductive rights, and domestic violence, then slap a girl if she didn't earn enough.

Life has a way of grinding a man down. George "Baby Face" Nelson died in his 20s. Al Capone died pushing 50. Bugsy Siegal died at barely 40. And John Dillinger, barely 30. No fair-minded person would call me a gangster. But these men, like me, lived too fast and too hard, and it all ended in a bad way. What did these men think while dying so young? Was it worth it? As my back warms the tombstone, what I could have been if this life hadn't forced me to do certain things? If Maria hadn't died, would I have been a world class racecar driver? Would they have put my name next to Paul Newman and Steve McQueen?

Maria wouldn't agree, but all my time spent driving and killing couldn't silence the thought of the futility of it all. Of time and death. These are the thoughts a man has when left alone with his own mind. Do all of us end in catastrophe, only for it to be repeated over and over? Is time linear, or a circle?

Maybe there aren't happy endings for anyone. In the end, don't saints and sinners all end up in the same place? Does it matter if you're gunned down like Baby Face Nelson, or flayed to death like St. Bartholomew?

As for me, my life's been a skipping record needle, playing the same broken tune of violence, and degradation. Threatening people. Beating people... *Killing* people. And just when the needle starts playing right, someone stomps the floor too hard. A man's face can only suffer a boot before he loses his soul.

"If you're out there, I think I did a final good thing, ya know? Elizabeth is a hell of a girl, but I think you know that." I paused, staring at the throbbing vein, lighting my last cigarette, and inhaling. "You may not be proud of everything I did, but in the end, in my final deed, hopefully you'd be proud." I inserted the needle and pushed down. "This whole world seems like teardrops in the rain." The wind picked up and stung my eyes. The crow squawked again.

I puffed harder, and my eyes transfixed themselves on the beast. In California, maybe things would be different. You have a big, beautiful heart, Maria used to say. She saw something in me I never could. But outlaws have wounds that fester, and no antibiotic prevents sepsis of souls. Mirrors become cruel, cracked and smeared with bile and all that remains are decayed husks tattooed to empty souls.

"Sorry I'm breaking my promise. I just…I just…"

It began snowing as I drifted in and out. The crow squawked again, and I took another drag.

"You were the only thing that ever mattered," I said. "I love you, Maria."

I took a final drag before the cigarette fell from my fingers. The crow flew off.

My breathing, and heart slowed. The snake bite was oblivion, contorted me into something other than myself. A numb serenity overtook me.

"Maria…I…I…"

The snake bite was like a mother's warm hug.

The snake bite was like Maria's first kiss.

"I…I…could have been so much more."

My eyes grew heavier, then I felt nothing.

Everything fades to darker shades of gray until everything turns black.

Chapter 2

My black 1950 Cadillac Sedan idled as blood soaked through knuckle bandages. If you'd asked me two decades ago if I'd be thrust into a world like this, Maria would've given you the finger before heading to a race. But, if my 47 years on this intergalactic ghetto taught me anything, it's that a man's calling is never what he imagines. Rarely do our interior lives mirror reality. And for a guy like me, existence is a game into a game of knuckle-crack-bone. An existence where hearing gunshots doesn't cause flinching.

But this is my last ride, which afforded a midnight conversation with myself. What is the American dream? Like many of us, it turned to a nightmare, instead of a life filled with radiant love, it's one of bone scraped over concrete. My life hasn't afforded many moments of contemplation, but in the dead of night, alone before the final ride, chaining cigarettes, and drinking whiskey, half-baked existentialism soaks my mind.

Waiting for the client, my hands throbbed and the night bled silence, as though the town took a night off from degeneracy. Staring at my twisted hands, at the mitts that once caressed a woman, that clutched a steering wheel, are now thick and meaty. The knuckles broken, over and over. And in the biting cold, arthritis reminded me of their function.

My car, this car, is still reliable. A memory from a previous life, from a time I'd both rather forget, but also cling to if only for the only good memories. One of the few remnants of a life not marred by senseless violence. A life where dreams were big, and futures brighter. A life filled with racing sponsorships, a loving woman by my side, and making love till dawn. A life devoid of smashing dudes and digging desert holes in the dead of night.

How it survived my time in prison I never found out. I can only assume Henry took care of it. Maybe he planned to use me all along.

Sitting here, waiting, I'm still trying to piece together the past. A vain hope I'll find meaning or redemption, perhaps. But my mind is like a jigsaw puzzle in a blender. Maybe it went sideways when, on a good day, my father broke bottles over my head. On a bad day, he gave me the wrench. Maybe my existence was doomed by being born to the wrong people. Perhaps Maria was just a reminder of what people other than me get to enjoy.

I yanked open the glove compartment, grabbing a roll of gauze and tape, needles and Smith and Wesson shells spilled on the floor. Goddamn it. If Maria could see the needles or shells, she'd level me with her eyes. I wish I knew why I kept the needles, having been clean since making the vow. Perhaps the needles formed a memory fragment of what life had been before Maria. A reminder of the homelessness, of destitution, of living off people's trash. A reminder that no matter how loud the demon's howled, heroin made them scream louder.

My revolver was a reminder of a life before Maria was my control switch. How, before her, pistol whipping dudes for sarcastic comments landed me in jail. How I'd broken a man's arm in three places for selling me low grade heroin. How once I put it to my head, pulled the trigger, only to realize the chambers were empty.

Riddles pile up in anyone's life, some we resolve, most just go around and around like a circus wheel. As each year passes, a little more escapes my understanding. The radio would fill me with messages of allegedly scary Black Panthers. I'd met a few, and they seemed more scared of me than the inverse.

Nixon declared a war on drugs last year, but anyone with a functioning brain could see it was a war on poor people. He also said hippies and feminists were American enemies, but they seemed fine to me. Word on the street is the guy's involved in some kind of scandal about breaking into the DNC. Too bad I won't be around to see how it turns out.

A man in a three-piece gray suit approached and knocked on my window.

I cracked the window. "Can I help you?"

The man held a hand over his mouth.

"Sir?" I asked. "What is it?"

"You don't know me," he finally said. "You saved my daughter's life."

"You must have me mistaken for—"

"She worked for Esmerelda. I'm sure that rings a bell?"

I nodded.

"Anyway, thank you. I want you to know she's safe. She's doing well."

"Good to hear."

"Whatever happened to Esmerelda?" he asked.

I lit a cigarette. "Rumor has it she's dead."

"How?"

"She's dead, and that's that." I rolled up the window and the man sulked away.

The man entered his house. My father's voice rang in my ear. He's a bad seed.

**

As I said, my father was a mean drunk, so I get why he beat me with a wrench. My mother was a whore, and given my father, who can blame her? I was a ghost to her. But I never figured out what Maria saw in me. Maybe at the end of this ride, I'll figure it out. Maybe in the end, it'll all make sense.

Christ, my knuckles throbbed more than usual, the busted hands of an aged laborer still too dumb to realize this is as good as it gets. What would Maria think of me now? Would she scold me? No, knowing her, she'd embrace me like an angel when we first met.

A faded wedding photo on the dash was my only reminder of a life before the symphony of violence. A reminder to stay off heroin, that H is just short hand for *death in installments*. A reminder that the reaper would come, but not now, not until this last ride.

This ride is important for some reason. And my gut rarely lies.

I finished wrapping the gauss taut, and stuffed the old rag in my pocket, and waited for the client, another girl, with a story told dozens of times. The kind of girl Maria once was, a black sheep in middle class America, the personification of the American nightmare.

"Cheatin' prick!" a woman yelled, storming out of a house. Her husband followed.

"It's not what you think," he said. "I promise. Just come back inside."

It shouldn't shock me that domestics happen in this neighborhood. No doubt a slap would come next, and she'd be ready to explain it away as a fall down stairs. Everyone would know it's a bullshit lie, but they'd play along because it fits a Leave-It-To-Beaver narrative.

Sometimes the girls I drove looked to me for salvation, but I'm no priest, and God don't roam these streets no more. In my world, a cacophony of prostitutes and crooked cops, pimps slapping girls, the sounds of women being raped, detectives throwing beat downs on black folks for the crime of I-don't-know-what. And all this was supposed to be normal. What an odd juxtaposition to see Andy Griffith on the tube at night, and then seeing a man like him sodomizing some poor bastard in broad daylight. Yeah, the world just don't make no sense no more. Maybe it never did. Maybe youth just gives an illusion of clarity, then you get older and realize how wrong you are about everything. Contra Poe: A nightmare within a nightmare.

The man and woman shuffled back inside before too many lights came on.

***

The girl slumped in the backseat, the rearview mirrored dead eyes and quivering lips. A stranger looked back and I couldn't tell if they were hers or mine. In this line of work there are no pleasantries. No hellos or goodbyes. That's for cabbies and limo drivers. That's for regular folk who work 9-5, have mortgages and kids. My line of work is akin to a mortician. Nobody wants to see us, and everyone pays us to be husher-uppers.

The girl was blood smeared over cracked mirrors, a crucifix hung around her neck like an albatross, bones pultruded through skin, a basketball in her stomach. Broken dreams and shattered promises sucked air from the car, as though she had Born to Lose tattooed on her from conception. Like all the others, sadness was her song. Looking back, she was like the other cracked mirrors. Most were quiet, ashamed, and preferred to blend in like New York beggars howling into the void, existing between a plane of existence and annihilation.

The urge to ask these girls their story never faded. Countless girls rotated through my car, and I longed for something happy. Something to restore my faith in the human condition. I almost always held back. Not for lack of empathy or sympathy, but sometimes there's too much pain and suffering for the heart to bear. Sometimes reality is too real, and it's best not to think about their discarded lives. Their truth is pimpled and bruised, reflecting a world where they shiver and suffer alone. A world where stern lectures are substituted for gentle words. A society hypnotized by simple, easily digestible narratives, swiftly interrupted by commercial breaks.

Does your husband beat you with a broom handle? Not to worry, maybe it's time for a Winston break?

This is The Twilight Zone - everyone's normalized.

I suppose these girls aren't much different from me. None of us have the luxury of Leave-It-To-Beaver- Truth. A world stripped of makeup. A world where drugs and alcohol are the last respite when hollow words, empty narratives, and phony people fail to produce anything of substance. A world with its skin ripped off, its liver-colored musculature of a corpse rotting under the setting sun.

Like me, these girls represent America's schizoid psyche raptured in cognitive dissonance.

"Sir," she said, "you ok?"

In summer, this girl's neighborhood would contain fresh painted fences and morning cut lawns. Suited men would buff cars and drink beers, while their wives sipped tea on porches. The older ones would stumble about with bottles of red wine and cigarettes lit at the wrong end. The dead end on the road to middle class America. The all-American dream, represented by polished exteriors, its secrets seared to the walls of each room.

What goes on in these homes? Does the man beat his wife? Is the woman screwing the mailman? What secrets do the old ladies harbor? Reality is more interesting when you imagine people aren't as dull as they seem. The real horror is often they are more horrific than imagination conjures. I see a suited gentleman enter his house, and I wonder, how many women is he holding captive inside? While in prison, my cellmate spun a yarn about his old man doing such things. The suit had white hair, so maybe his secret is he's a banker and helped fund The Third Reich. Then again, maybe he's just as boring as the rest of barbiturate-induced America.

"Sir," the girl said again. "Are you ok?"

"Yeah, sure," I said, remembering I'd zoned out. "I apologize."

"Ok, it's just you've been staring out of the window since I got in."

"Sorry about that."

She cracked a smile. "It's okay, just wanted to make sure everything was fine."

I nodded and shifted into drive. "I'm fine."

Leaving suburbia, I sped down a careless highway, knuckles still throbbing and head spinning. With my record, a crooked cop would stop me at any moment. They all wanted a handout or information I didn't have. Sometimes a seasoned prick, or a bored rookie unable to find a black guy to unleash his rage on took it out on me. You know the type. The kind of guys who became hall monitors and idolized their high school principles. Some became president, some got their body bags zipped by men like me.

Driver

Sciatic pain slammed my brain. My right leg burned and tears rolled down my eyes. Not sure what injury caused this, but it had to be my right leg. Goddamn it. Time to pull over.

"Are you sure everything's ok?"

I grabbed my leg. "It's fine. Just, ummm, gimme a few."

"What's wrong with your leg?"

"It's…fine. Just…" The pain made me trail off.

"Ok, let's take your mind off it. What's your name?" The girl rubbed her crucifix.

"Driver."

"No, silly, not your occupation. Your—"

"Driver."

She leaned forward, tears welling up in her eyes. "Can you make all this easier on me? Please?"

Maria would know what to do. She had the touch of a mother's warmth. She could melt steel with her smile and turn a guy's legs to rubber with a flick of her hair. What could a man like me say to ease her humiliation? Would I say everything will be alright? She knows that's bullshit and haven't we all had enough of that red, white, and blue bullshit rammed down our throats?

There's no anesthetic for the brokenhearted. But here she was, comforting me, and expecting it to be reciprocated.

Goddamn my leg burns. Guess I'll have to plow through and hope it doesn't go completely numb. "I'm just your driver this evening, and your appointment's in two hours. I'm gonna get you there on time, ok?"

The girl gazed out the window. "Oh, ok. I see."

"I promise."

"Ok."

"Just hang on." I rubbed my leg a bit more as if that would help. "Just…gimme a second."

"You sure you're ok, sir?"

"Yeah, fine. I just. Just. Few minutes here. Please?"

"Sure, yeah, ok. Sorry."

"It's ok. No need to… no need to… apologize."

Judging from the neighborhood, girls like her came from families who played The Convent Game. Simple rules: Shuffle them to a convent for a few weeks, tell congregations, or other interested parties the poor darling's in a hospital, or visiting relatives, or temporarily ran away, or hooked on reefer. Almost any lie will stick, after all, if only they found Jesus, all their problems would be solved.

The pain wasn't going away, and I don't dare take pain killers. But the glove compartment looks tempting. No. Not now. Not yet. My senses must remain sharp.

On the days Maria dragged me to church, it amused me how the priest would use the word immorality to refer to sexual transgressions, or the phrase living in sin. If you're John Dillinger, robbing banks and killing people, you aren't living in sin, but if you give blowjobs behind a dumpster you're living in sin. It sounded ridiculous coming from my father's mouth, and from a priest's. Too much moralizing, too little good will. But running your mouth like a phone bill is easier than putting in the work.

I'd sit in church with Maria, staring at the half naked man nailed to a cross and muse about how an organization against homosexuality represents themselves with a homoerotic symbol. The irony wasn't lost on Maria, and sometimes she'd chuckle, other times she'd tell him to be silent.

I never bought the holy shtick of priests. They want me to believe someone accepted a vow of chastity? A red-blooded male would refrain from sexual congress? We're humans, sure, but deep down we're controlled by the reptilian brain. The priests were either banging the nuns or raping the altar boys. Sex is like cards. Solitaire is fine, but a man needs poker.

Maria's attraction to Catholicism escaped me, and she never gave a satisfactory answer, usually resorting to: we all need something to believe in. Maybe that's my problem. There's nothing for me to believe in. Maria told me Victor Frankl claimed a man with a why could suffer any how. Is this why she handled her death with such poise? Few people live with dignity, let alone die with it, but she managed both. Wish I'd been there to witness her end.

"Sir," the girl said, "you really don't seem well."

"Please," I said. "I'll be fine."

Maria liked rituals, as she was a creature of habit. But not traditions or rituals handled down from corporate America or society, but traditions the two of us cultivated together. She refused to celebrate Valentine's Day, saying it robbed romance of the surprise. Every Christmas we'd make a new ornament for the tree, and every Saturday we'd read passages from her Bible.

Though cynical about religion, it's hard to say no to an angel stolen from Heaven.

The sciatic nerve acted up more and more, burning pain setting my leg ablaze. My bones throbbed, and my heart bled. Without Maria, what's the point of going on? After all these years, and countless tears, grief infected my soul. It's time for a permanent vacation.

"Please don't worry," I said, rubbing my leg. "I'll get you there safe."

She nodded and smiled. "I know."

"How?"

She cocked her head. "I sense you're a good man."

If only that were true.

Chapter 3

In our third year of marriage, doctors diagnosed Maria with breast cancer. They tried reassuring her about treatment options. Ever the optimist, Maria believed them. As for me, well, optimism isn't in my constitution. Maybe it's not in my DNA, or maybe my father beat it out of me. At this point, does it matter?

Too many people give into false hope. My first day on the streets I sat next to a WWI vet missing both legs. He chatted my ear off, and an older woman approached and gave him a dollar. She said everything would work out. But she didn't know his wife divorced him after the war. She didn't know he lost his house shortly after when he spent all his money on booze. And she didn't know he'd been out here since the late 1920s. But even after 20 years on the street, the man smiled, assured that any day his luck would change. That it was only a matter of time before God smiled on him and made everything alright.

I never got the man's name, but he seemed like an old friend with a resigned smile. We shared what remained of his bottle and I shared cigarettes with him until the sun went down. The old timer fell asleep and never woke up.

The streets were filled with people drunk on hope, then they'd get shot, stabbed or overdose. After a few months, the streets stripped any hope of a better life. Once you see a cop pistol whip someone to death after seeing two pimps gun each other down, you see the world as it really is - a wretched place anathema to humanity.

Maria seemed to be getting better until July 8th of 1952 when the doctors said she had stage 4 cancer. So much for advanced medicine and cutting-edge treatments. By

September, with all the chemo and radiation, she could barely move from her hospital bed. She'd become a skeleton of her former self, hairless, ribs protruding through the skin, eyes that contained a faint light of the sun before.

We'd always dreamed of sailing the Pacific. She wanted to feel the California breeze on her face, the sand between her toes and relax next to a beach fire.

"Remember," she said a few months after we were married. "You still owe me a proper honeymoon. I've always wanted to taste the pacific winds."

Seeing her now, guilt overtakes me. Why didn't we go when she was first diagnosed? Between races, she never asked, but I could see it in her eyes. She wanted to go. I guess I figured there'd be time later. Maria has a way of filling a soul with hope for a better tomorrow.

Between hospital visits, I sat on our porch drowning my liver. Retreating to the garage, I'd eye the empty spot where my Ferrari 340 America had been. I told Maria I'd saved up while working at the track. The truth is, I stole it. No way a mechanic's salary would ever buy such a work of art. And now it's gone. Sold to pay for some of Maria's care. But it wasn't enough.

"Mr. Malone," Dr. Harris said, "we've exhausted insurance options and you're behind on payment. I don't mean to be—"

"How much?"

"We'll need our first payment by the end of the week."

"How much?"

"$5,000."

"Two weeks ago I sold my Ferrari 340 America. I gave you $9,000."

"Sir," Dr. Harris said, "I'm sorry. I really am. Mrs. Malone's treatment is expensive. And—"

I glared at him.

"Yeah, glare at me all you want. I know you want to punch me. Do it. I know what you are. What that nice woman ever saw in you is a mystery."

I lit a cigarette and inhaled. "Your treatment's not working."

"We're doing the best—"

"With the $5,000, there's a chance she'll make it?"

"Slim, but anything's possible. The best is to make her as comfortable as possible in these last weeks, maybe days."

I inhaled fire into my lungs. "You'll make her comfortable, right? You promise?"

"You have my word."

"Fine. I'll get the money," I said, gesturing to a window. "If you don't, I'll shove your fuckin' head through that window."

***

Maria's last days consisted of priests visiting her cancer ravaged body. She said they brought her comfort, but I wish they'd leave me alone with her. But in they'd keep shuffling.

The oils,

The holy water,

The incense,

The robes,

The Last Rites…

…And the crucifixes. The endless fuckin' crucifixes.

They all felt the need to etch a Last Rights Prayer onto my brain:

Loving and merciful God, we entrust our sister to your mercy. You loved her greatly in this life; now that she is freed from all its trials, give her happiness and peace forever. Welcome her now into paradise, where there will be no more sorrow, no more weeping or pain, but only peace and joy with Jesus, your son.

"Mr. Malone," Father Vincent pulled me into the hallway. "Has Maria atoned for her sins?"

"Guilt her, and ye'll leave on your back."

"Mr. Malone, my son, you seem troubled. And I understand the—"

"You understand nothing. Leave it at that."

"My son," he said, "what can I do?"

"Listen, Maria needs more money, ok?"

"Our parish donated all it could."

"I know you don't like me," I said. "That's fine. I get it. But that woman in there? She needs $5,000. She's the best this world has to offer."

"Mr. Malone, I'm sorry, we don't—"

"She doesn't need stupid fuckin' prayers to your stupid fuckin' God, ok? She needs money for treatment. Period. End of fuckin' story."

"I don't appreciate—"

I balled up Vincent's collar. "Did Jesus die so altar boys could suck yer filthy fuckin' pecker?"

Vincent tried pushing me away, but I kept my grip, staring into his fear fueled eyes. "A preposterous accusation," he said. "How dare you."

"I know 'bout you. I know 'bout the last three congregations you worked. How much did the Vatican pay for your victim's silence, you fuck?"

"You don't know—"

"I know you were at The Vatican when they turned Jews away," I said.

"You go to Hell."

"Guilt her, and I'll deliver you there." My eyes pierced Vincent's, letting silence echo through the hall, I could almost feel the priest's heartbeat. "Either cross my palms with Dead Benjamins or get the fuck outta here. We clear?"

"Crystal."

"You sure?" My breath was on his neck. "I need to be sure we understand one another. Maria likes you, but I'd just as soon send you to the morgue."

"Let me go."

I shoved him down the hall. "Just remember what I said."

***

Incense burned while other priests chanted scripture in mechanical Latin. A dead language, read by dead eyes, interpreted by dead mouths, for an almost dead woman. I couldn't understand a damn word of it, but Maria understood

Latin. She tried teaching me once, but only two phrases ever stuck: Semper Fidelis (always faithful), and Ab Imo Pectore (from the bottom of my heart).

"Ricky," she said after they'd left, "Could I trouble you to read some in English? My eyes aren't so good right now, and I like the way you read it."

I'd nod, caressing her paper hands, the wedding ring dangling from bone. "Of course. Anything, sweet- heart."

"And Jesus said unto him, verily I say unto thee, today shalt thou be with me in paradise." (Luke 23:43).

Over the weeks, I'd memorized Luke 23:43. Something in those eighteen words, arranged just right, brought a strained smile to her face. I'd read it, eyes glazed over, mouthing the words, its resonance numbing.

"I know you're not religious, but if it's not too much to ask, could you read another, Ricky? Please?"

A waterfall was kept locked behind my eyes.

"Darling? Please?"

"...And God shall wipe away all tears from their eyes; and there shall be no more death, neither sorrow, nor crying, neither shall there be any more pain: for the former things are passed away." (Revelation 21:4).

Maria wept enough salt to create a second Dead Sea, though not for her inevitability, but for me. She never said it, but I knew she worried about me. In our short time together, she'd done so much for me. She felt responsible for my well-being. She wanted more scripture, I just wanted to walk with her on the beach.

"Think I'll go to Heaven?" she asked. "Think we'll be together in the afterlife?"

"I'd like that very much." A tear dropped from my cheek. "If anyone deserves paradise, it's you."

"It's alright darling." Maria caressed my arm. "I know you can go on without me. You're stronger than you know. You were the best thing in my life."

I melted in the chair, every muscle became rubber, every tension loosened and for a moment, the world evaporated. Back and forth, she touched me as a mother should. Her touch was like that first hit of heroin almost a decade ago.

"I love you, Ricky. And I know you love me. You gave me my best years, even if it was only a few." She paused and smiled. "I always saw your heart. I saw it immediately. Someday, I hope you see what I see."

I lit a cigarette, and in silence, she drifted in and out of consciousness. A deeper kind of sadness took hold of me. The kind that doesn't go away. The kind that lingers and haunts you until your final breath.

"Promise me you won't give up your dream," she said. "Promise me you'll be a famous race car driver. Ok, Ricky? Can you promise me that? Can you promise you'll at least try?"

I covered my eyes and turned away.

"Ricky, baby, you'll be ok. Hey, listen, remember when we met Paul Newman? I never saw you smile so much." She let out a laugh. "And who can forget Steve McQueen? You said they'd be big one day. I bet you're right."

I shrugged.

"I know it's hard to ask, maybe it's an impossible request, but don't mourn me too much, ok? We are all blips on this strange little planet. It's amazing, isn't it? I could have died before I ever met you. I could be here, right now, alone. But

I'm not. I'm here with you." She had a resigned smile. "I wouldn't change any of it for the world."

"I need you longer." I teared up. "I...I just..."

"It's hard to let go." Maria clutched my arm. "In time, promise me you'll find someone who loves you like I do."

"We promised never to lie to each other."

"Do it for you, and if not you, do it for me, ok?" She placed the wedding ring in my palm. "Find someone, Ricky, and touch her with your beautiful, gorgeous, giant heart." She paused, gasping for air. "And darling, please, for me, and for her, stay clean."

I fled, collapsing in the hall.

Chapter 4

A week before my last ride, I sat on my steps watching the sun set, chaining cigarettes, and nursing cups of coffee. December 7th would be my last ride. I had a client on the 4th and another on the 7th. Doing what I do, with the life I lead, makes a man pushing 50 feel twice that.

I was about to start in on Miller's *Tropic of Cancer*, when Tommy, a scrappy Irish punk, perhaps late twenties with busted knuckles and jagged teeth, approached again. Pimps said Tommy was getting in on the numbers racket. Hookers said he tried getting into prostitution, but the bosses gave him a concussion. This guy would hit me up every few weeks with some screwball idea guaranteed to get innocent people killed.

"Got a proposition for ya, Ricky," Tommy said. "Gimme a smoke, too, or I'll smack ya upside the fuckin' head."

I tapped the revolver hanging from my belt. "I ain't a smoke shop. Now make like a tree and fuck off."

"Hey, don't get fuckin' fresh, Rick," Tommy said. "You'll like this."

Rumor had it that Tommy pulled off a few bank jobs. Local branches, but he had a thirst for something more lucrative. Cash may be king, but Tommy complained about the weight.

"Bags musta weighed 70 muthafuckin' pounds," he said. "Fuck that. Precious gems, Rick. Precious gems are where it's at. Been scopin' this place out for weeks. Wholesale fuckin' diamonds comin' in tomorrow. But I need a driva' if things go south, ya feel?"

"Find someone else. If you really knew me, you'd know I'm the wrong guy for this job."

"Hey, do me a solid, Rick," Tommy said. "You came highly recommended by Henry. Do me right, I do you right."

I snubbed my cigarette and lit another. "You deaf? Find someone else."

"15% cut, Rick. Tomorrow, at noon. Keep the car runnin'. I know this nice place. Real fuckin' nice. Like I said, wholesale diamonds. I promise you'd get, well shit, at least $2,000." He threw up his arms. "Easy money. Things go as planned? We drive away all nice an' peaceful like, and you get an easy 2K."

"Shut your mouth," I said, "or I'll shut it for you."

***

I stuffed his body and a shovel in the trunk of his 67 Mustang and began my drive to the desert, with plenty of time to think. Night turned into morning and I stopped for gas, then continued on.

I'd been out this way plenty of times, and each time wondered why I didn't just leave. Just drive another day to the Pacific. Henry'd be none the wiser, and I doubt anyone would put up much fuss.

I didn't know how to sail, but figured I'd learn. Maybe set off and make it to Hawaii. Perhaps that's where the land of peace was. Sitting on a beach, sipping drinks, maybe even opening up a sailboat business.

I finished burying Tommy by noon, deep in the Nevada desert and sat on the hood of his car as the sun baked down. I stared down the empty road - I could be at the Pacific by sunset.

Maria would call it intuition, some call it a gut feeling, but I had to go back. She'd always tell me; You don't need to know the *why*. It's a hell of a thing living with the ghost of someone else in your skull. But her ghost never led me astray. My

27

problem was, I rarely listened. Staring off into the distance as the sun paints the horizon, I wonder - would things be different in another life? Are we all condemned to repeat the same things over and over? A teacher told me those ignorant of history are condemned to repeat it. But we know history is one of brutality, and we still do it. What's the point of knowing history if it's stuck on repeat?

I lit a cigarette, hopped back in the Mustang and headed back. "Ok darling, I trust you. A last ride."

Chapter 5

Silence around others is unbearable to most, but not as much as driving with the phantoms of bad memories. The six-hour round-trip brought me a strange solace, a kind of detached resignation. Getting beyond the city, away from the lights, away from the ceaseless chatter of people, the gunshots - the unending cruelty was almost sublime.

"Not a radio guy?" the girl asked.

"Not really."

"I was always told the radio was the work of the devil."

Why couldn't my last ride be quiet? But as always, like a bartender, I often acted as a makeshift shrink. We'd just left the confines of the city and started a short stint down farm country. My leg still burned, but one learns to live with such conditions.

"Well," I chuckled, "if radio is the work of the devil, and pardon my language, sometimes he fuckin' rocks."

I looked in the rearview and she cracked a smile. "Back in 69, my friend Mary and I went to a Zeppelin concert."

"Zeppelin?"

"I think they'll be really big."

"I wouldn't know."

"Not a music fan?"

"Not really."

I paused. Should I keep the conversation going? Maria would want me to. "What did your parents think?"

"They're squares." She paused. "My dad especially. He was a boy when The Nazi's invaded Poland. That's where he's from. He is constantly worried about the moral decay of this country."

"I was a teen during WWII." I paused, lighting a cigarette. "Mind? Want one?"

"It's fine, but no. Not now."

"The moral decay of America, eh?" I asked.

"Yeah, I guess it left an impression on him."

I wish I didn't know what I know. I wanted to tell her this country has always been one of moral decay. That the game is rigged. That I'd read too much in prison, saw too much on the streets, and seen too much driving to wave the red, white, and blue. I wanted to tell her American banks funded The Third Reich. Hell, I went to one client's house, and her banker's dad, on his deathbed, spilled all the secrets of what American banks did. I wanted to tell her how Hitler admired America's slave system. I wanted to tell her so much, but I think she already knew. I suppose my gut told me she didn't have much faith in the American system anyway, so what's the point? Why pile on more misery to an already miserable soul?

"War changes people," I said.

"What about you? What do you remember?"

I remember most people smoking opium, while I saw others shooting heroin. I remember my father hitting me with a wrench after finishing his bottle of Jack Daniels. I remember a concussion from being thrown down the stairs. I remember my mother wishing she'd found someone to abort me. I remember my first overdose at 15, and my second at 16. And I remember being thrown out of the house on my 17th birthday.

"You know young men," I said. "I was mostly causing trouble and chasing women."

She chuckled. "Like my older brother. My aunt had a way with him, though. Or so my parents said."

"Like she hit him with a stick?"

"No, silly. I don't think. She could calm him, I guess. I never met her, but I heard a lot of stories." She hung her head and took a long pause. "Thanks."

"For what?"

"Talking with me."

"You sure the smoke don't bother you?"

"It's fine. No really, thank you."

"No problem," I said. "How old are you?"

"How old do you think I am?"

I sighed. "Trick question. I learned a long time ago never to guess a woman's age."

"C'mon," she leaned in. "It's ok. I won't get offended."

"18?"

She clapped. "Very close. 16."

"Too young."

"Hey," she said, "your knuckles. What happened?"

"Nothing good."

"Wanna talk about it?"

"No."

Chapter 6

It's trite to say but holds true regardless - the first of anything significant scorches itself on your memory. I remembered everything about the day and night of the Kennedy assassination. I took three good shits, my prison food didn't have the usual number of maggots and I felt refreshed after getting out of a 90-day hole punishment.

I sat down with my tray, and the radio announced Kennedy had been killed. I was 38. Most prisoners fell silent, but a lifer who went by Crooked Eye Bobby didn't seem to care and never gave me a consistent answer on his age. Sometimes he said late 50s other times early 60s. Either way, he'd been here since 1928. Rumor has it he killed his whole family, but I wager he was more into armed robberies and moonshine tax evasion.

"Yo, Rick, I missed ya."

"Well, Crooked, old Warden Wallace don't like heathens."

He slapped the table and let out a laugh. "He try pushin' that Bible shit on you again?"

I nodded.

"Man, please tell me you earned that extra 30 days."

"Earned?" I smirked. "I told him to shove his Bible up his fuckin' ass. Those words."

"Good." Crooked took a bite. "Fuck that mother- fucker."

Few days later, guards beat him and left him for dead overnight. I never saw the poor bastard again, so I assume he died.

This brings me to my third memory out of prison.

A few days after release from prison in 66, after putting flowers on Maria's grave, and after meeting Henry, Kleopatria entered my car. She was like a stripper on Broadway, a tapestry of broken promises painted on yellowed canvas, with a cashmere coat and an evening gown and, though dolled up like a geisha girl, the makeup couldn't hide the gash on her cheek or the dent in her chin. Truman Capote was right: Americans hate non-egalitarian beauty. Maria told me that.

One didn't have to be Sherlock Holmes to realize high end prostitution was her game. I think they call this "escorting." The kind to go for captains of industry, or senators. And the kind that if you crossed, consequences would be wetted out bloodless violence leaving pieces of your life scattered across the country.

Prison taught me to size people up, and Kleopatria was a siren type, like Monroe. She could weave a fantasy web and seduce and control any man. As Crooked said: Beware the siren. They are hypersexual, confident, mysterious, and stink of danger. That, lad, is their allure.

It wasn't until weeks later I discovered she used to be a French model. After moving to the states, her manager dropped her after a guy slashed her cheek. All this was in her obituary.

Kleopatria finished the joint and flung it out the window, her Chanel overpowering the atmosphere.

"How lovely, darling. Henry got himself a new whore. Hope you're not like the other jerkoff."

"Close the window. There's a draft."

She lit a Pall Mall and inhaled. Smoke filled the car. "What's yer story?"

"I drive."

33

"Ya musta fucked up to get in with Henry." She dangled the cigarette between her fingers. "A natural born loser if I ever met one. But he's got a good scam going, risky workin' with Italians though."

"If you say so."

"The world's one big whorehouse, driver. Ya fuckin' face looks like a hangover. The body don't lie, darling. What broke ya?"

The siren who lost her call. All the trappings of a siren distorted by time and jaded by people like me.

"Listen lady," I said, "how 'bout we have a nice peaceful ride, ok?"

"Wife?"

"No."

"Kids?"

I slapped the dash. "Hey, whatd'I say?"

"You must have some story. They all do. And they all spill their guts. The johns—"

"Ya gonna psychoanalyze me now? Ya Sigmund Freud? I ain't a cheap trick, and I ain't yer fuckin' john."

"Mine? no." She cracked the window again and winter flooded the car. "I ain't Freud, nor Jung, nor Skinner, or whomever the fuck else, but I sure as fuck don't need a degree in psycho-fuckin'-therapy to see right the fuck through ya."

"You talk like this to clients?"

"Of course not." She took a long drag. "Well, some like being degraded. That's different."

"You're not as dumb as your makeup. You're lucky I don't carve you up and worry 'bout the consequences later." I started the engine. "The window. Close it."

"You wouldn't. You're no mystery to me. Picture of your wife on the dash. Helping out us poor little damsels in distress. You one of them save the world queers?"

I reached back and cracked her in the jaw.

Kleopatria whipped the blood from her lip and took another drag. "The real question, the one that keeps you up at night, the one which haunts your waking nightmares, and the answer that alludes you is—" She paused. "Guess."

I raised my hand. "No. Close the window."

She twirled her gold engraved lighter. "What shattered you? You don't belong here. What series of—"

I gestured to a payphone down the block. "Shall I call Henry?"

"He's too busy getting sucked off by an associate of mine." A black widow cracked her face. "Oh darling, you really don't belong here. Truth be told, I don't either, but the world is a hell of a thing, ya know? You go through life with this model in your head of how life should go. Then the world turns the wheel a hard left, speeding toward a cliff."

I gripped the steering wheel.

"Ever read Camus?" she asked.

"No."

"The Myth of Sisyphus is mostly a Dostoyevsky and Nietzsche circle jerk. But—"

"Lady, I really don't care."

"This whole world is a theater of the absurd. Do you revolt? How lost do you get in your own mind? You go through life, doing the same—"

"Christ woman, you have an appointment. Shall we shove off?"

She took a drag, then another, and flung the butt out the window. "I dunno, shall we Big Boy? Or do you smack me around a bit more? Last guy who did that ended in a bad way."

"I'm sure he did."

"Read much?"

"Maria did."

"Who?"

"Doesn't matter." I turned the key and the engine hummed.

She lit up again and smoke clouded the car. "No one dies a virgin, darling. Life fucks us all."

I shifted into drive. "Yeah, great, I'll be sure to cash that at the bank."

***

The first time I waited in a car I forgot to bring a newspaper. Maria would suggest I bring a book, and since Kleopatria brought up Camus, she'd probably suggest The Stranger. After reading it, she said anything else by him would be garbage in comparison.

Some people aren't structured for book learning. Some are born to drive fast cars. My first race was down a dirt road when I turned 15. Some punks wanted to race. I'd like to say I won, but I ended up wrapping my old man's 39 Chevrolet around a tree.

After the paramedics patched me up, I got the wrench and a return trip to the hospital. Second time my old man gave me a concussion but the first time he broke my arm. He died a few years after kicking me out. Not soon enough I'd wager.

Kleopatria exited the mansion, drenched in sweat, her face like a ghost.

"We're done."

I started the engine.

If she ran her mouth going there, she didn't say a word on the way back. She dozed in and out of consciousness.

I pulled up to her house.

"The Stranger," I said. "That's what Maria liked."

"Pardon, darling?"

"The book. She liked it. Maria, that is."

"Yeah." She paused long enough for silence to permeate skin. "She has good taste."

"Except in men."

I could tell she eyed the picture. "Sounds like you really care for her."

I nodded. "She was my angel."

"Was?"

"Was."

"I see. Well, life never works out as planned, does it?"

"Sorry for hitting you."

She waved the voice away. "It's fine. Don't worry about it. And thank you for the ride. You're a good man. I can feel it."

"I dunno about that."

She opened the door. "You have a nice evening. I'm sure I'll see a lot more of you."

A few days later, after my second cup of coffee and before my morning shit, I saw her obituary. Found dead in her home dangling from a rope, blood from her uterus pooled on the floor. It outlined her modeling career from 1955-1958. Apparently for those three years, she was all over French magazines, until she moved to the states and the world forgot her. She was 28.

For some reason I attended her funeral. In the coming years, this would become a ritual. After the first dozen, one tends to forget. The state buried Kleopatria to a crowd of one. For all the glam and glory she once had, for all the men she serviced, for all the fame she garnered in France, nobody showed up except me. Sitting outside, the priest gave a eulogy. I imagined this is how Maria's went.

A wooden box and a piece of granite off the side with just these words:

Esme Anais Dupont

Nov 22nd,1938 - Dec 15th, 1966

No saying. No quote. Just that. A woman's short years on this planet summed up by nothing more than a name and a date.

The next day, a letter with a tattered copy of Camus' The Myth of Sisyphus arrived in the mail with no return address.

Dear Driver,

I want to apologize for how crass I was during our trip. Since you're reading this, you've probably deduced I'm dead.

I wonder, did you attend my funeral? I wonder if anyone did? Though our time together was brief, I meant what I said. You're a good man. As for me? Well, I've reached the end of my road. Camus once said the only important question is whether or not to commit suicide. But I'm not Sisyphus, and no longer can I push my boulder. Luckily, I don't have to. You'll see I sent my French version of The Myth of Sisyphus. Though it's doubtful you can read French, I hope it'll serve as a token of my appreciation. At least someone can remember me. I'll leave you with what my father said before swinging from barn rafters.

Mon travail est terminé et maintenant je passe à autre chose.

(My work is done and now I move on),

Kleopatria.

The book remains on my nightstand, next to my revolver.

On days Henry doesn't ring, sometimes I swing by the cemetery and place flowers on graves of girls I remember.

Someone needs to remember.

Someone needs to care.

Chapter 7

The morning my wife died was the afternoon I sat outside a bank waiting for two men to bring out bags of fat stacks. With medical bills piling up, who could turn down the promise of a successful score? I'd met two men while weeping outside the hospital, unable to bear the suffering of my beloved.

"I remember you," Thomas McCain said. "Yeah, back in, oh shit, 51 I think?"

"Hell of a driver," Richard Maslow said. "Saw you thrown up against a pig's car after that street race."

"Wait," Thomas said, "Were you the sumbitch who beat Fat Frank?"

"What do ya want, guys?" I asked.

"Can you still handle the wheel?" Thomas asked.

I lit a cigarette. "How 'bout you boys run along now."

"We got a proposal," Richard said.

"Good for you." I waved my hand. "Scram."

"Hear that, Thomas? We got a tough guy here. We're offering this faggot a—"

I chopped Richard in the throat then slammed Thomas to the ground. "Fuck off before I rearrange your faces."

"Christ man," Thomas said. "Three-way split. Our last fuckin' driver bailed. We gotta move."

I clutched his throat tighter and his eyes bulged from his skull. "You try to fuck me on this and I'll have your body bags zipped."

"Ain't like that, man," Thomas said. "Wells Fargo branches. Decent scores, and all within a three-mile radius of one another."

"Dumb shits," I said, "You don't talk this shit among decent folk."

Richard leaned in. "Listen man, each branch is loaded, ok?"

Thomas leaned in. "I got inside men on each branch."

"How much do I get?"

They said there'd be around $10,000 at each location. With a three-way split, Maria would continue receiving care. The bank was foreclosing on our house. As luck would have it, the one branch we'd hit was the same one foreclosing on us.

***

"Sweetheart," I returned to Maria's room. "I have something to do real quick."

"You ok, Ricky?"

"I'm fine. Rest up and I'll see you in a few hours."

"Ricky, I don't feel well. Will you stay?"

"I'll be back. I promise."

She clutched my arm. "Please?"

"Two hours tops. Ok?"

"Promise?"

"Promise."

"I love you, darling." She clutched my hand. "Return to me."

I kissed her forehead. "I love you too. And I will."

"Ricky," she said, "when I get better, can we see the Pacific?"

There ain't no getting better. "Of course."

She smiled. "Now come back safe, ok?"

I nodded.

The boys lounged on benches, recovering from the beat down. "I got rules."

"Oh?" Richard asked.

"We do this, and when it's done, it never happened. We clear? You gimme my cut, and if you ask me about the job even five seconds later, I'll deny it. It never happened."

"We're not stupid," Thomas said. "We'll keep our mouths shut."

"And when do you open your mouth?"

"At the dentist," Richard said.

"You get caught," I said, "You don't know me."

Both nodded.

"And if either of you think of runnin' yer fuckin' mouths? Well, I'll cut your tongues from your heads."

"Whatever, whatever, what the fuck ever, guy," Richard said. "We doing this?"

"We're clear?"

"Yes," they both said in unison.

"Good," I said. They gestured to a souped up 52 Buick Roadmaster. "Ok, let's go."

***

The boys walked out and slumped in the car. Four bags loaded with cash. The dumb luck was, there was a cop in the area and before I could hit the gas, a woman ran out screaming.

"Don't shoot, motherfuckers," I yelled to the boys.

They listened and I squealed tires. It wasn't long before a parade of sirens followed behind us. Soon, the gas tank went from full to half.

"This is fuckin' bad," one of them said. "They ain't fuckin' lettin' up. C'mon man. Fuckin' go."

The other punched my seat. "Faster, asshole."

I pulled out a revolver and pointed it at him.

"Silence or I'll nuke you motherfucker."

"Faster cocksucker!" Thomas said.

I cracked him in the mouth and he spit out teeth. I took a hard left then a hard right down a suburban street. Silence. White fences. A brief vacation from the cops.

"Fuckin' Christ," Richard said. "Thought you could handle the wheel you dumb shit."

"We shoulda shot that fuckin' pig while we had the chance," Richard said.

I got out, and drug the two men onto the street, my revolver pointed at them.

"We need that money too, bitch," Thomas choked through blood.

43

I kicked him in the stomach. "You think I give a fuck what you need? Talkin' about smokin' cops? Fuck you both."

Richard lunged at me and I dropped him with a kick to the groin. "Tired of your yapping." Sirens blared in the distance. "Enjoy the cops, cocksuckers."

I got back in, to the yells of: You're dead! You're fuckin' dead!

After that, everything became a blur until I lost control down a country road and crashed into a tree. In hindsight, Tommy was right about the weight. There were four bags, and I couldn't possibly haul all of them.

By noon the dogs were on my scent in the woods. Two bags and my knees were getting weak. I collapsed, staring beyond the trees, into the sky. The coroner's report said Maria died a little after noon. While the cops were dragging me out of the woods, the medical people were taking her down to the morgue.

Before her last breath, I'm told she said:

Where's my Ricky?

***

They took me down to a smoke-filled interrogation room. From the other room I heard variations of *confess, nigger!* followed by smacks and howls.

An interrogator came in, coffee and cigarette in hand and took a seat across from me. "Hear that, boy?"

"I'm not deaf."

He lit up and took a drag. "Your confession can go one of two ways."

"You'll beat me regardless," I said. "You want a confession? Earn it."

"Nah," He wagged his thumb towards the room next door. "That nigger don't know his place, that's why we're here to help him. But I think you're smarter."

"Maybe. Maybe not. Maybe go fuck yerself."

"We got ya dead to rights, Mr. Malone. The money was on ya. Truth be told, we don't need a confession, but it makes things easier." He slid a paper across the table. "Sign on the line, asshole."

"Ok, sure. Right after you go fuck your mother."

"Value the integrity of your nose?"

"That it?"

"Clearly you didn't do it alone."

I shrugged. "Maybe I did."

"And maybe a phonebook breaks yer fuckin' nose, smart guy? Or maybe when sentenced, I spread word to the warden you like touching little kids."

I shrugged. "I don't know what you're talkin' 'bout."

"Doesn't have to be that way, Mr. Malone. The way we see it, we got two other knuckleheads. One poor bastard's hospitalized. Another was shot in the back, maybe you did that. Read between the lines." He paused, taking a drag. "But I gotta good feelin' about—"

"So you want me—"

"Listen, the D.A. is willing to give you 13 years. That's fuckin' generous given your miscreant past." He inhaled smoke. "But, and this is a big but, you need to name the other two men and testify."

"Ok, on one condition."

"Pal, this is the best we can do." He leaned back. "I got guys in the can doing decades for less."

"I want to see my wife one last time."

"Maria Malone? Sorry pal, she died this afternoon while you were out fuckin' around. You'll have to live with that. Her last moments were spent alone while you terrorized the fine folks of my fuckin' community."

"I want to attend her funeral."

He took a long drink and stared into my eyes as smoke curled around his head. "No can do. This is the offer. Take it, or I beat yer ass, and you die in the can. And I'll make goddamn sure everyone knows you like little girls. I can be your best friend, or your worst enemy."

I picked up a pen. "So that's that?"

He got up to leave. "I'll give you five minutes to make up your mind."

In prison I learned Thomas and Richard were much like me. Though we never met after, as Thomas went to the morgue, and Richard to a different prison. But prison walls speak volumes.

"Yeah man," I heard from my cell. "Thomas McCain and Richard Maslow. Some asshole really fucked'em over."

"How so?" another voice asked.

"Man, these two fuckin' guys were some of the unluckiest sons'a bitches I ever fuckin' met."

"Go on."

"I knew 'em. Good fellas, but not mob types. Just good boys. They fell into a bad way. Real bad way. They only planned those robberies to pay for diabetic medication for some broad."

"A broad? Like a hooker?"

"I dunno. All I know is they both liked her or some shit." Long pause. "It wasn't sexual. I think they were queers or some such. Regardless. She couldn't pay. She needed medication. That's why they did it."

"And this person who fucked em?"

"No clue. They have some code of honor. They won't rat him out. Some bullshit about Omerta."

"Huh?"

"Some mafia code of silence or some bullshit. But they're not even fuckin' Italian. And to the best of my knowledge, never did mafia work."

"So why Omerta?"

"I don't fuckin' know, man. Maybe they think it sounded cool."

"Listen kid, in here, keep yer mouth shut. Not a bad policy."

"Nobody likes a rat, eh?"

"I overheard an Italian once say; snitches get stitches and wind up in cement ditches."

I tried falling asleep the first night but couldn't. Tears wanted to flow for Maria, but my eyes wouldn't allow it. I did get a lucky break with my cellmate, though.

Driver

"You'll be alright," a voice said in the dark, "What are you in for?"

"Tell you tomorrow," I said.

Chapter 8

Red and blue lights flickered in the rearview. Officer Martin again. I'd say he was crooked, but to last in this job, you gotta take envelopes. Corruption and sociopathy are correlative to power advancement. Some guys just take payoffs, while others find twisted enjoyment in the torment of others. Last week Officer Martin shoved a broom handle up a negro's ass. The guy bled out on the street while bystanders passed by. Rumor on the street was he couldn't afford the Martin-style shakedown. Some say Martin was slinging reefer on the side, others say he had his hands in prostitution, but there was evidence of neither. As best I could tell, he just enjoyed extortion with the occasional handcuffed beatdown.

The girl turned pale. "Is this bad?"

"Happens all the time. I'll handle it."

The girl clutched her crucifix. "Ok."

Snitches don't get stitches, nor end up in cement ditches, instead they get cops shakin' them down every time they think, maybe, perhaps you may have jaywalked. Some demand drugs, others information, but all threaten.

A good day is avoiding a broken leg.

A good day is just a laundry list of questions.

Do you know who [insert name] is?

Do you know where to find [insert same name]?

Do we need to take you downtown?

A phonebook to the nose, and car batteries on the scrotum became the new normal.

I rolled down the window and curled my lip attempting a smile. "Officer Martin, a pleasure as always. How's the—"

"I won't ask for your license and registration," he said, "but yer left taillight's out."

"Damn, Officer, I apologize. I'll make—"

"A man's vehicle is his castle, Ricky boy. This is a beautiful fuckin' car. Whadda thinkin', guy?"

"My bad, Officer. I've been goin' through—"

"Yeah, sure, fine, just get it fixed." He leaned in closer, the smell of Aqua Velva penetrated my nostrils. "While I got ya here, know anything bout Tommy 'The Fist' O'Sullivan? Word from above says he's a new player in town. Heard anything?"

"Can't say I have."

"Nothin' at all?" Martin rapped his fingers on the hood of the car. "Gimme sumpin', Ricky boy. Be a damn shame if we had ta bring ya downtown again." He winked. "I doubt you fancy car batteries outside the engine."

I lit up and gazed in the rearview, the girl massaged the crucifix. "Word has it he's an enforcer for a Mafia outfit, not The Gambino's, rumor has it, Carlo Gambino ain't doin' so hot. Perhaps The Winter Hill Gang? Maybe The Bufalino's if he's goin' big, bout all I know." The fire burned my lungs. "Wish I could be more helpful."

"A fuckin' mick tryin' to get in with the Italians?"

"Probably with The Winter Hills. I don't pay much attention."

"Lotta rumors, no solid info?"

I shrugged.

"Nothing solid?" Officer Martin asked.

"Just rumors." I white knuckled the steering wheel, inhaling more fire. "And like I said, I don't hear much these days, Officer. Hell, I never really did."

Martin winked. "Right, sure, if you say so, bud."

"We done?"

"I'm trying to make detective. See, there's a string of doctors and med school dropouts winding up dead. Shot. Stabbed. Bludgeoned." He paused. "Real sick shit. Long shot, heard anything?"

"Not to be rude, but time's ticking, Officer. Jim Morrison's dead, and I ain't feelin' too good myself and because of your bullshit the girl's gonna be late."

Officer Martin glanced at the girl. "Knock some broad up, eh, Ricky boy? She looks young, like some high school broad. Here we all thought you turned queer after bein' sent away. Ain't never heard'ova rubber dumb shit?"

"We?" I asked. "You were still shitting your pants when they sent me away."

He waged a finger at me. "The old timers remember, and they talk. Tell me about the girl."

"Hey," Rick gritted his teeth, "bad choices and all."

"So my ex-wife says. Dumb bitch will—"

"With all due respect, Officer, we're already late for a doctor's appointment."

Martin rapped the hood. "Get the fuckin' taillight fixed for Christ's sake."

"Officer," I said, "as much as I enjoy our frequent conversations, they need to stop."

"The fuck you think—"

I grabbed a folder from the passenger seat and threw it at Officer Martin. "It'd be a damn shame if this was made public."

Officer Martin paged through, his grin turning sour. "You think you can—"

"Shall we talk in private?"

***

Officer Martin snorted a line of cocaine on his hood and we both leaned against the cop car, the lights still flickering, cars whizzing by. The winter air hung and the stars made their presence through the flickering clouds. Such a scene reminded me of Maria and our long walks in the dead silence of winter. Even when the cancer ravaged her body, she still convinced me to go on these walks against doctor's orders. I suppose it was something about the silence she knew would bring me peace.

In the early days, sometimes I'd lean against a pole and watch her dance along the sidewalk. The universe gave the wrong one cancer.

Officer Martin was green, only on the job a few months, but made a habit out of following me. Most cops rotated pulling me over, so not much value in digging. But after six times in two weeks? I made it a point to dig, and found a pot of gold. I made it a point to make sure the next time would be the last.

"This is a dangerous game, Ricky."

"You know my reputation, and you know there's a lot of holes around here."

"Oh, threatenin' an officer of the law?"

"Pull me over again, and I'll make sure you fill a hole." I finished the smoke and flicked it. "And I won't like it, I really won't. You seem like just a run of the mill dumb shit cop." I paused. "I'll feel bad on my deathbed."

"How bout I arrest you right the fuck now?"

"Go for it, then send your men to search my apartment. I wonder how Commissioner Morgan would like photos of you nailing his wife? And, word has it he's mob connected, though I bet you know that." I gripped Martin's shoulder. "Now I'm late, so you're lucky. You wasted my time, which usually results in payment of flesh. A broken bone, busted noise, a concussion. But I'm a nice guy today. How 'bout you, Officer? Are you a nice guy today?"

Officer Martin gritted his teeth. "You won't get away with this."

I lit another cigarette. "In the end, nobody gets away with anything."

"You'll see your dead wife soon enough."

I thought about shoving his face through the driver's side window. Fire boiled inside me, and if I didn't have a girl with me, he'd walk and talk funny the rest of his life.

My eyes bore into his. "Don't see me later, peckerwood."

***

Walking back to the car meant an explanation to the girl. Perhaps she even turned back and looked and wondered why.

I got back in the car. "Sorry about that."

"What happened?"

"You didn't look back?"

"Too scared."

"Why?"

"Officer Martin," she rubbed her crucifix. "Well, he and I go back. He probably doesn't remember me, but when I was a girl I walked in on him sexually assaulting my sister."

I started the engine and proceeded down the road. What did she want me to say? What could I say? Patronize her? Tell her everything's going to be ok? Fuck. It's better when they don't speak. I wish once, just once, one of them had some kind of happy story. That's unrealistic, but a man can dream.

"Do you believe in forgiveness?" I asked.

"What do you mean?"

"I dunno, I guess, move on in some meaningful way?" I asked.

"Of course, I've had to do it quite a bit. Do you?"

"I think forgiveness is shorthand for forgetting. Maria thought I should forgive. Never could. Doubt I ever can." I pause. "But my memory fades each year. So that's something."

"Who?"

"Sorry, I ummm, nevermind. I'll stop."

"It's ok."

"You're Catholic, right?" I ask.

"Yes sir."

"I'm more of an Old Testament type God."

She laughed. "I doubt you're that much of an asshole."

"Yeah." I smiled for the first time since Maria's death. "You and Maria would get along."

"The woman you don't want to talk about?"

"Correct."

In all the rumblings I almost forgot about my leg. When pain is constant, you tend to forget about it, or if not forget, become accustomed. But as silence set in, my leg began going numb. And the memories always flooded back when the booze wasn't flowing.

I caressed the picture of Maria. A tear rolled down my eye. Was this more than a last ride? Maybe this is what Maria meant when she said find someone else. Not romantic. No. Something more. My finger couldn't locate what, but this girl was special somehow.

"Rick," I said.

"What?"

"Rick Malone."

"Your name?"

I nodded in the rearview.

"So, you are more than just a driver." She let out a chuckle. "You do have a name, eh?"

"I, ummm…"

"It's ok. I know men like you. Taciturn. Reserved."

"I don't usually do this."

"Well," she said, "I'm Elizabeth. Elizabeth Hart. Beth for short. Whichever you fancy."

Chapter 9

Cops and the general public don't realize bank robbery is a victimless crime if done right. The pure act of taking paper we've all agreed has value does but one thing: increases the money supply, which the government can print on whim.

But we live in a world crafted on the philosophy of John Locke, don't we? Property possesses more rights than people. Prison gave me plenty of time to read. Plenty of time to think. Plenty of time to talk with others.

"I was a teen when they shot John Dillinger," Mack 'Dapper Desperado' said. "His mistake was killin' people."

I'd read about Mack in the papers when he was sent away in 1942. From 1938-1941, he and his crew were rumored to have robbed dozens of banks, often several in the same day and in different states. The incident that got him caught was a three-pronged heist. Morning: Citibank in Chicago. Afternoon: Wells Fargo in South Bend Indiana, and on their way to Ohio, him and his crew were boxed in.

"Greed got us," Mack said. "We all got used to steak dinners, fancy wine, and even fancier suits."

"How long you in for?" I asked.

"Well, shit, until they take me out in a body bag."

Crooked smirked. "They nailed you on how many robberies?"

"Fuckin' bullshit," he said. "Some other crew was robbin' another bank in Chicago and pinned that on us."

"Three?" I asked.

"That's right." He paused. "60 fuckin' years."

"Yup," Crooked said. "No parole either."

"Listen," Mack said, "and listen carefully. Don't get the wrong impression about me. My crew was tight. We never harmed anyone."

"What happened to your crew?"

"Well, let's just say cops shot em, alright?" He turned his gaze at me. "And you? How'd you fuck up?"

"Wheel man."

Mack's face lit up. "Ah, experienced?"

"First time."

"What's yer story?" Mack asked.

"Wrong place, wrong time."

"Yeah, no shit. Why'd ya do it? Not a 9-5 jerkoff?"

"For my wife." I lit a cigarette. "I just wanted to be a race car driver."

"Shit man," Mack said. "I just liked living like a movie star."

"Listen Rick," Crooked said, "The warden's a real prick. Did you take the Bible he gave?"

"Yeah."

"Probably a good idea to find Jesus," Mack winked.

"Just memorize some passages, and you'll be alright." Crooked said.

***

Driver

In prison everyone seemed to find Jesus, except my cellmate, an elderly Japanese man Amida Takahashi. Nobody quite knew what he was in for. Some claimed hit and run, others said he beat a guy to death in a bar. But he was nice to me, so I didn't care much. The man spoke little in the few years I knew him. He never badmouthed anyone, and when he did speak, it was often in riddles.

"Fit the sun in your pocket." Silence would ensue. How the hell do I respond to this? Then he'd follow it up with, "Why did Bodhidharma go to China?"

"I have—"

"These are Koans," he said. "Don't answer. Meditate on them."

"A Koan?"

"Your cup is full of opinions." He'd pause. "A Koan cannot be explained before you empty yourself."

Above his bed, written in Japanese, he said was the Heart Sutra. On the night of his death, he took three breaths, then expired. In his hand was a translated version for me. I don't remember much of it. But one section stuck with me.

So, in emptiness, there is no body,

No feeling, no thought,

No will, no consciousness.

There are no eyes, no ears,

No nose, no tongue,

No body, no mind.

There is no seeing, no hearing,

No smelling, no tasting,

No touching, no imagining.

There is nothing seen, nor heard,

Nor smelled, nor tasted,

Nor touched, nor imagined.

Perhaps this stuck with me since the prison library had many of Nietzsche's works, and I'd later find out this German philosopher was an early western admirer of Buddhist philosophy.

What does The Heart Sutra mean? Who the hell knows. To me, it sounded like nihilism with a happy face. A Polish inmate handed me a piece of paper, claiming the following was an excerpt from Philipp Mainländer:

"But at the bottom, the immanent philosopher sees in the entire universe only the deepest longing for absolute annihilation, and it is as if he clearly hears the call that permeates all spheres of heaven: Redemption! Redemption! Death to our life! and the comforting answer: you will all find annihilation and be redeemed!"

Can't remember his name, though he wasn't well liked. While most of the others read their Bibles, he'd drone on about human extinction. If I had to speculate, I doubt he ever really enjoyed life. And as far as I can tell, he had contempt for the cosmos.

A few weeks after the note, guards found him dead in his cell, hanging from rope he crafted from his sheets. No note, and nobody was surprised.

"His brain didn't work," Crooked said.

"You owe me two packs," Mack said.

"Bullshit."

"You bet me he wouldn't do it."

Crooked threw two packs at him. "Fine."

My years in the can were mostly boring. When not in the laundry, I'd be in the library, or chatting up Crooked or Mack. Sometimes I'd be sent to the hole. Sometimes we'd have to shank a pedophile. But mostly I remember walking the courtyard, keeping the memory of Maria alive.

"By my records," the warden said, pulling me into his office, "you're set to be released next month."

"Yes sir."

"Enjoy it, I'm sure I'll see you soon anyway."

"You won't."

He puffed a thick cigar. "I will. You people never change. Politicians run their mouths about rehabilitation. Gets em votes." He leaned back. "Know how many people I see return?"

"With all due respect," I said, "I don't give a good goddamn."

His face turned red, and he gestured to a guard. "Take this cocksucker to the hole for his last month."

"Fuck you. Fuck your Bible. And fuck your whore of a mother!"

The guard beat me good then drug me to the hole.

That's about all I care to remember from my years in prison.

Chapter 10

The day they paroled me, I took a bus to the cemetery and arranged carnations on Maria's mostly barren grave. She never talked about her family much, now I know why. There was a waterlogged unsigned note from one of her nieces.

Dear Maria,

I never knew you, but my dad tells stories. I think you would have been a great aunt. I understand why you cut the family off. Dad can't bring himself to visit you, but he's sorry for everything. I keep leaving these notes every few months, and I don't know why. Maybe it's because I don't have friends. I keep asking dad about your husband, but he walks away. I wonder what he was like?

Love,

A Nobody

I welled up knowing at least one other person cared about Maria. She never let me meet her family, and when pressed, would respond *the past is where it belongs.*

Sitting in the graveyard alone, I gave myself permission to grieve. I never really processed her death in prison, and even now, my heart refuses to accept she's gone.

"I'm sorry," I said through tears. "I'm sorry I never took you to the Pacific. I'm sorry you died alone." I caressed her tombstone. "I'm sorry for the way I am."

"Mister," an elderly woman said, extending a piece of cloth. "Need a tissue?"

I waved it away.

"She doesn't get many visitors." The woman gestured to the grave. "I come here every week for my husband Jerry. Sometimes I see a small girl. You know her?"

"Afraid I don't, ma'am."

"She's sweet. So full of life. Remember those days?"

"I'd rather not."

"Ok, mister, I'm sure I'll see you around. I need to go see Jerry."

Maria would want me to forgive myself. She'd probably say it's hard to ask, but beg me not to mourn her, but celebrate the time we had. But I just don't know what I'm doing on this planet. My life began and ended with her.

"I've let you down, Maria. Many times. But you wanted me to keep going, didn't you?" I paused. "Ok. I will. For a while at least."

***

The following morning, I reported to the parole office. The room sweated bourbon and reeked of stale cigars. A smoky haze hovered above, the kind of room you'd expect public defenders to occupy. The last respite for losers who probably had to be juiced in to avoid selling trinkets from a tin cup. In hindsight, I wager even Henry could fuck that up.

"R. Malone, right? Cigarette?" Henry Johnson asked.

"Yes sir, but I don't smoke anymore." I took a seat.

I sat as Henry thumbed through my file, chaining cigarettes, and slamming glasses of Johnnie Walker.

"Helluva a deal from the D.A, Rick." He let out a cough and hawked mucus into a bucket. "Yes indeed. Helluva deal.

Hell'va file, too." He looked up. "Bet your parents are real proud."

"They're dead, sir."

"Yeah, well, I don't feel too good myself." He hawked more into his can. "Illegal racing at 16, eh? And kept doin' it. Got brain damage or somethin'?" He puffed harder. "Busted over and over for fights too. You fuckin' degenerates never learn."

"Sir, I'mma play it straight, I promise. I'm a changed man." I opened the newspaper. "I've even got leads on work, ads for cabbies, limousine drivers, a few garages are—"

"Fuck all that." Henry poured another glass. "They don't want some peckerhead like you."

"Sir, with all due respect, I called Jimmy's Garage. He's—"

"Oh yeah? He know about your record?"

"No."

"I know Jimmy. He don't want some fuckin' criminal workin' with decent people."

Life is too short to be good at too many things. Hell, it's hard enough becoming good at one of them. My racing dreams fell apart, and frankly, I wanted nothing to do with automobiles. Sadly, life doesn't allow much in the way of reversal, does it? They say you can reinvent yourself, and maybe there's truth to that, but I knew cars, and I was too fuckin' old and too fuckin' tired to reinvent my wheel. But I knew cars and wasn't much good at anything else.

I flipped to the ads. "I have a dozen or so others circled. I can show—"

"Rick." Henry slammed the glass down, "Did you hear what I fuckin' said? Decent people don't want your kind. We clear?"

"Sir, with all due respect, I think—"

Henry threw the file across the room. "You sold your rehabilitation story to the parole jackoffs. Good for fuckin' you."

"I wasn't paroled. I served my full sentence."

He banged his fingers on the desk. "You people. You bloodstains on American society set up for me to clean up."

"If you'd look, you'd see lots of ads for—"

"You know how long I've been doing this?" Henry snubbed his cigarette out and lit another.

"No sir."

"Before your balls dropped."

"Ok?"

"And you know what I learned?"

"How to be a Grade A fuckin' asshole?"

"Fuck yourself," Henry said. "People don't change, Malone. They pretend, like most of the people in Hollywood pretend they have talent. Like Elvis. His music the stuff for niggers, and his movies are even worse. Ya know, I'll give folks like you this. Ya try. Many of ya really do try. But ya don't change. The crimes change you. Crime sticks to you like glue."

"I really think if you look—"

Henry cracked a window. "Fuckin' Christ, you'll drive, alright? A special kinda driver. I'll set things up, give you the time and place, and you be there, ok? I take 70%, and you get the rest."

"I ain't a wheelman no more. A cabbie? I can do that. And I know cars. In prison, I brushed up on manuals. I'm sure a garage—"

Henry crushed his cigarette on his desk and leaned over. "Listen here. You do what the fuck I say, or I make one phone call and yer sweet little DA deal is null an' fuckin' void. Back to the fuckin' can for hard fuckin' time. Time so fuckin' hard you'll think ya got fucked by a train." Henry dangled an unlit cigarette from his lip, sweat drenched his forehead. "Ya work for me. Ya don't fuck with decent people."

There's a rage a man feels being under the thumb of another and it boils over when the boot can't be removed. Without a government title, I'd have broken Henry's face and thrown him out the window.

"Yes sir," I said, white knuckling the chair.

"Good, I'll call you in a few days." He lit up again, and smoke poured from his nostrils. "Now get the fuck outta my fuckin' office, faggot."

"Say that again, you'll drink out'va straw."

Henry bolted up and threw his glass. "How bout I call the DA?"

I flexed my meat hands. "Pick up the phone, and I'll see you in the ICU."

Henry crashed in his chair. "Just fuckin' wait for my call."

"I need 50%."

"Get the fuck outta here."

"It's 50% or I break yer fuckin' jaw." I leaned in. "See Henry, here's the deal. My wife's dead. My family's dead. And you've read the file, you know I'm comfortable with violence. Surely you understand I have very little to lose by turning you into a cripple?" I paused, my eyes piercing his. "Two men in the can will never walk right. Me and the guys shanked pedophiles and rapists. Get my drift?"

"40%," he said.

I pointed to the window. "Know how to fly?"

I got my 50%.

I made around $250 most months.

***

After my first week, Henry met me in a smokey lounge playing Jazz.

"Good work," he said. "All three women made it back safe."

I ordered a scotch. "No, they didn't."

"They all returned home, right?"

"Kleopatria committed suicide."

"So?" He ordered a martini and lit up. "She made it home."

"What kind of driver am I?"

"Why do you care?"

"Well," I said, "she was found dead. She was bleeding from the vagina."

"Shit happens," he said, downing his drink in one gulp.

"She was high class."

"Yeah. Was."

"What kind of driver am I?"

"I'm late," he slid a folder over. "This comin' week's packed."

Chapter 11

We passed cornfields and farmhouses in silence before entering a small town with a population sign that read 317. A church on our right, a gas station on our left. We blinked and it was gone. More cornfields. More open road.

"You're Catholic, I assume?" I asked.

"Sure, I suppose."

"You suppose?"

"My dad is," she said.

"And your mom?"

"She's a sucker for appearances."

"My wife was Catholic," I paused, still unsure why I was talking about her. "But I don't think she took it as seriously as she let on."

"Sounds like my mom," she said. "Your wife was Catholic?"

"Was."

"What happened?"

Images of the pacific oceans swirled in my head. How I'd dreamed of sailing with her after I'd made it big racing. We'd always said once we had enough money, we'd set up a little place in California and ride out this life with fruity drinks and a beachside bar, the ocean wind filling our lungs. Hardly a week passed where we didn't fantasize about it.

"Sorry," she said. Damn it. I must have paused too long. "I didn't—"

"It's fine. I just…"

"I don't want to offend."

I dangled a cigarette from my lips. "Sure you don't mind?"

"Mom smokes two packs a day."

I lit up, trying to ignore the pain in my hands, and the burning numbness in my leg. The last of anything is memorable, especially if you've been doing it for over six years. Gasoline was always in my veins. But these last few years turned it into napalm.

"I hope I don't offend," she said, "but you have broken bottles in your eyes."

"There's a lot that's broken."

"I'm sorry."

"Happened before you were born," I said. "Hell, I'm tempted to think it happened before I was born."

"I have an interesting theory," she said.

"Ok."

She perked up. "Nobody believes me. They all think I'm crazy. But I call it Birth Dice."

"Never much of—"

"Hang on. This is interesting. I promise." She leaned forward, a twinkle in her eyes. "Here's some facts. We didn't choose to exist. We didn't choose when to exist. We didn't choose where to exist. We didn't choose our parents. We didn't choose what we were taught." She leaned in. "See where I'm going?"

"Not really."

"We don't choose much of anything, do we?"

"I suppose we can choose our thoughts."

"But can we?" she asked. "Suppose you grew up to Jewish parents. You'd be a Jew, right?"

"I suppose."

"Maybe, but even that choice is determined by the influence of genes and environment, right?"

I took a long drag. "I guess."

"So, we're not really responsible for anything, are we?"

I let out a mucus-soaked laugh. "I can tell why your musings weren't well received." I chuckle. "Everyone loves blaming someone for something."

She made the haha sound. "Right? I spent a lot of time in libraries."

"Me too. At least for a while."

"Which one?" She perked up even more.

"Better not to say."

"Rick," she said, "I've only made it this long because I can read people. A prison library?"

I nodded in the rearview. "I read a lot of car manuals. But sometimes other books too."

"Why car manuals?"

"When I was a boy, I stumbled on a street race. I knew I wanted to be a professional race car driver. The speed, the sound, the cheers, the thrill." I paused. "Obviously it didn't work out."

"Someday, maybe?"

I flicked the butt out the window. "My time's pretty much passed."

"Rick, do you think it's possible to transcend who we were told we are?"

I started out in a cycle of violence and returned to it. You can take the man out of the streets, but not the streets out of the man. What has the world taught me? What has the world taught Elizabeth? At a certain point, it doesn't matter.

Cement covers my soul.

I forced a smile in the rearview. "For you, I hope so."

Chapter 12

A week after my first visit to Maria's grave, I returned in the hopes of finding the girl the old woman mentioned. The old note was gone, replaced by a fresh one.

Dear Maria,

The girls at my school keep diaries, but I don't see the point. I suppose these notes are a kind of diary, right? Lost to the winds. I really wish I could have met you. In my head, I imagine you doing all the things Dad says you did. Climbing trees and throwing rocks at random strangers. He even said you broke a kid's nose once when he bullied you. He has loads of stories. I hope someday I can be a free spirit like you. The rest of the family says you were a "whore," and a "heretic." I had to look those words up. It's my birthday today. Mom drinks a lot. I didn't get a cake. If you're in Heaven, I can't wait to meet you. Did you ever wonder if Heaven was real, or just a fairytale like Santa? I sometimes do. But I hope it's real, just so we can have fun together.

Love,

Nobody

The cemetery was empty again and only the wind and birds spoke. Maybe people more quickly forget the loss of their parents than the loss of their property. I sat there for hours, keeping the flame of Maria alive until a man approached.

"Mr. Malone?" he asked. The man with slicked back hair wore a gray suit with gray slacks, a gold vest and striped tie.

"Who's asking?"

"My name's Don Ricci." He bent down. "Heard of me?"

"Sorry."

He put a crisp $100 bill on my hand. "I want to discuss something."

"With all due respect, Mr. Ricci, I'm not a wheelman despite what you might have heard."

"It's not like that," he said. "Can we talk somewhere else?"

I looked at my watch. "I can spare maybe 45 minutes."

"Walk with me," he said. "I'll only need 10."

***

We took a seat on a bench overlooking a duck pond.

"Word has it you knew Kleopatria," he said, lighting a cigarette for himself then me.

"Knew is a strong word." I took a puff, first drag I'd had in years. "I was her driver."

"Regular?"

"Once."

"Why?"

"I don't know."

He took out a leather-bound notebook. "She was going to be the next big thing."

"Ok?"

"Hollywood. I could feel it."

"So you're some kind of agent?"

Smoke poured out of his nose. "I grease the wheels a little."

"Mr. Ricci," I said. "What's this got to do with me?"

"I cleaned her up. Spent a year, and a lot of money ensuring she'd be the next Marilyn Monroe." He puffed harder. "She was supposed to be a lead in Knock, Knock, Bang, Bang. Set to start filming—"

"Get to the fuckin' point."

"Watch your mouth, greaseball. I'll crack yer fuckin' skull," he said. "The point, Mr. Malone, is I want to know who killed her."

I exhaled smoke in his face. "Read the papers."

"I don't buy that suicide bullshit. Yeah, fine, maybe she hung herself. But why? And why was she bleeding from her lady parts?" He opened his wallet with more crisp $100 bills. "You drove her someplace, right?"

I took a drag and nodded.

"Good." He threw his butt into the pond. "Tomorrow, noon, meet me at Mickey's Tavern and take me there." He paused, handing me another $100 bill. "Let's just say: I'm connected, and you'll make another $300."

***

I drank two whiskey sours and smoked three cigarettes waiting for Mr. Ricci. I went to pay the bill and leave.

"It's on the house," the bartender said, fixing me another. "Mr. Ricci will be here."

"He's got till I finish my next smoke and this drink."

He tapped me on the shoulder. "Sorry I'm late, traffic's a bitch."

"If you say so."

He gestured me up and pointed to a Shelby GT350 Fastback. "Handle one of these?"

"You're late."

"I know. Can you handle it?"

"Does a priest enjoy the company of young boys?"

"Good," he chuckled. "Let's go."

We pulled up to the mansion I'd dropped Kleopatria off at.

"Your hands good?"

"Why?"

"Are your hands good?"

"Sure, why?"

He slipped $300 in my pocket. "I'm assuming you're not just another dumb fuckin' mick."

I glared at him. "We're in a car. Enough riddles. You need me to throw a beat down?"

He shrugged. "Hopefully not." He sized me up. "Good. Street clothes. I got somethin' nice after. Don't worry."

"Listen," I said, "my part's done. I took you here. Whatever the fuck you gotta do? Do it."

He gestured to his suit. "Just follow my lead."

"And if I say no?"

He removed a pistol. "You wind up in a river."

I pointed to a Lincoln Continental in the driveway.

"Yup," Mr. Ricci said. "Someone's home. Let's go."

Chapter 13

After a few months working for Henry, word spread that I was a reliable driver. Pimps with flashy clothes would hit me up for bodyguard work. Not my style. The kind of men who wore gaudy rings tainted with the blood of women who didn't pay enough.

Henry said I was exclusive to him, but after my parole, I needed some scratch for California. I was sitting alone in a nameless bar in a part of town best left forgotten.

"Sugar," a woman in a white silk dress said. "Bother you for a smoke?"

The evening was young, and I was only on my third cup of coffee. I lit her a cigarette and she took a seat next to me.

"It's getting late," I said. "This is a bad area."

"Rumor has it you turned down DJ Sparkles. He could have made you rich."

I stared into my cup. Nobody should drink this sludge. "I didn't like him."

"Nor I." She took a drag. "Why don't you like him?"

"Why all the questions?"

"I run a service, sugar. I'm very selective—"

I lit a cigarette. "Ok, well, I'll stop you right there. Not interested."

She touched my hand the way Maria used to. "I'm not like the others."

I winked. "You bet."

She extended her hands. Smooth. "I'm not like the others."

"Listen, I—"

"I didn't catch your name."

"I didn't give it."

"I'm prepared to pay you $50 per ride. And I have over a dozen girls. And they all work this like a 9-5."

"Building?"

"Correct. And the right pockets are lined. The others are blackmailed."

I finished my cup and cigarette. "Let me think about it."

"I know you work with that jerkoff Henry." She paused. "Mostly days?"

"Mostly."

"Good. We do nights." She extended her hand. "My name's Esmerelda."

"You wanted to know why I didn't like DJ?"

She nodded.

"He touches women in ways men shouldn't."

"I hate that cocksucker," she said, rage seething behind her teeth. "My girls are treated right."

"Good, because if they aren't," I clutched her arm. "I'm sure the streets tell other stories about me."

She nodded and wrote down the address. "Here. I'm here nights from eight to three. Seven days a week."

"I'll think on it."

Esmeralda leaned in. "Sugar, you wanna die poor? Don't think too hard."

***

In the heart of the city, down some stairs, stood two tattooed guards.

"Appointment?" one asked.

"I'm here to see Esmerelda."

The other towered over me. "That's not what I asked, dickhead."

"Step back," I said. "I'm Rick Malone. She's expecting me."

"I never heard of ya," the other said.

"Like I give a fuck what you heard," I said.

"Well, tough guy here."

"Ok," I said, pulling out a cigarette and lighting it. "Yeah, you two can easily pound my head. I'll lose. But." I paused, taking a long drag. "Before I lose consciousness, I'll break as many bones as I can." I blew smoke in his face. "Now get fuck outta my face and get Esmerelda."

The door opened. "What's the problem?" Esmerelda said in a red silk robe. She looked over at me. "Mr. Malone. Good. Come in."

The guards opened and let me pass.

The men turned white. "Sorry Esmerelda. We didn't know. We were—"

She held up a finger, her eyes cold. "We'll talk later." She turned to me, placing a hand on my shoulder. "Come in darling. Have a drink, and let's talk."

***

The place was fancier than most places I'd been. An underground haven for degenerates with class and style. Velvet couches, Bach played softly, and the girls moved with an air of delicacy, but authority. I'd heard in the Wild West women like Esmeralda commanded towns. Women like her had the power to make or break politicians. Women like her had all the dirt to make sex a woman's power.

I took a seat at the bar while Esmerelda said she had some things to finalize.

"What's yer poison, sir?" the bartender asked.

"Whatever's least expensive."

"Mr. Malone," he said. "No worries. Esmerelda said you'd come around and said to take care of you."

I smiled. "I'm a sucker for a classic. Gimme an old fashion."

"Yes sir."

I drank two old fashions and watched the girls interact with the clients. Their subtle seduction game. I was the only guy not in a tailored suit. Before Esmerelda came down, I observed three girls, and of three guys, one was a state senator I recognized. Robert Whitlock. His face was all over the papers about family values, preaching how we need to clean up the streets of prostitution, and drugs. He claimed Nixon endorsed him, but that was unsubstantiated.

I waved the bartender over. "That's Senator Whitlock, right?"

"Yes sir."

I took a drag and laughed a little.

"Mr. Malone, he's the tip of the hypocrite iceberg. You'll see."

"I'm sure I will."

Esmerelda appeared and motioned me to a booth. The bartender brought her a martini and gave me another old fashion.

"As you can see," she said, "most of our work is in house."

"Why do you need me?"

"Some clients pay very well for more private experiences."

"At their homes?"

She nodded. "I need to ensure their safety."

"I just drive."

"That's not what Mr. Ricci said."

"Christ, that fuckin' guy needs to keep his fuckin' mouth shut."

She looked me dead in the eye. "Don't worry about his mouth."

She slid me an envelope. "Count it."

$300.

"Consider this a good faith gesture." She waved over a girl. "This is Kofi. Kofi, this is Mr. Malone." She waved her away.

"When do I drive?"

"Drive and protect, Mr. Malone." She gestured to the bartender and he brought over a briefcase. "Inside is a Magnum, gloves, and other necessities."

"When?"

"Finish your drink," she said. "It's 9:13 right now. The client wants her by 10."

Esmerelda told me new clients need a strong introduction. As she explained to me, girls come to her with the promise of safety. While Esmerelda can vet clients, one never really knows the devils that lie within their skins. The more we spoke, the more she spoke my language.

"Remember, Mr. Malone, respect is based on the ever-present fear of violence." She paused. "The men need to know this."

"Understood."

She grinned. "I know, I know."

She clicked her watch and slid me an address. "I expect a strong introduction from you."

I nodded.

***

Kofi sat in the back. For the first half of the drive, she didn't say anything.

"Your eyes bleed sorrow," she said.

"Pardon?"

"Inside you," she said, "there are two wolves."

"Ok."

"One is love. One is hate. They dance around and around. Which one wins?"

"The one you don't feed," I said.

"No, the one you feed."

"A starving wolf is a desperate wolf. And a hungry wolf battles harder. This is why they starve fighting dogs."

She chuckled. "Well, my cleverness fell flat."

"Cleverness is overrated."

"Ya know," she said, "folks have my kind all twisted."

"How's that?"

"See," she said, "they think all of us are junkies, or had terrible parents, or come from defective cultures. Ask any of the psychoanalysts." She paused. "Truth is, sure, yeah, some of us are that way. But it's also true that many of us like it. Hell, it beats a regular 9-5." She leaned in. "I bet you pegged us all for dumb broads, eh?"

"No," I said. "Judgements are a luxury I don't have."

"One of these days I'll have enough scratch to really be free, ya know?"

"Ok." We pulled up to the mansion. "Stay here. I need a word."

"Whatever you say, cowboy."

I rang the doorbell and a bath robed man with a glass of amber liquid and graying hair answered.

"Can I help you?" he asked.

"Esmerelda sent me."

"Is there a problem?"

"I hope not." I pointed to my car. "Kofi is inside. After we understand one another, I'll bring her over."

"Understand what?"

"She exits your house safely."

He makes an expression of bourgeois offense, "I don't appreciate your tone."

"Here's the deal," I said, "if I see even a scratch on her? I'll blow yer fuckin' brains out."

"That a threat?" he said.

I stepped closer. "Want me to break your jerkoff arm?"

"Ok, ok, relax."

"Not. One. Scratch."

He nodded. "Of course."

I slumped back in the car. "Scream if you need me. And let me know if he does pull anything, ok?"

"Okie dokie."

"How long's he got you for?"

"30 minutes."

"In 31 minutes, I burst through the door."

"Thank you."

I nodded.

I cracked the window and lit up. Strange being in such a neighborhood. All the 9-5 people. The doctors. The lawyers. The CEOS. The politicians. All the people with money. Why do people do what they do? Pure instinct? Is there a semblance of rational deliberation? After all these years, I thought that I wanted to be a racecar driver. Maria showed me there was more. The more I drove, the more I realized I just didn't want to be poor. I wanted a slice of the American dream the flag promised.

The neighborhood was quiet and I relished it. No gunshots. No fear of running over a dead body. No fear of a shake down.

After my second smoke, before I lit a third, the girl ran out of the house and slammed the car door. My watch indicated she'd been inside 23 minutes. I looked back and saw a busted lip and black eye.

"Let's go," she said, holding back tears.

"Stay here, ok?"

"Yeah."

There was a payphone around the corner. I grabbed the gun and put it in my belt and headed over there.

"Esmerelda," she said.

"We got a problem."

"Go on."

"Kofi has a busted lip. And a black eye."

"Fuckin' cocksucker." She paused, her tone turned ice. "Listen carefully. Make sure he never walks or talks right again."

I hung up.

I ran to his house and kicked in the door.

"Get the fuck—"

I cracked my fist into his nose until he dropped. I took the butt of the gun and slammed it into his jaw until I heard a crunch and he spat out teeth.

"You dumb motherfucker!" I said. "I fuckin' warned you."

A few more cracks to the skull, and I jammed the gun in his mouth. "You're only alive on the good grace of Esmerelda." My hands shook. "Left up to me you'd leave in a body bag."

"Ambulance…" he choked out.

"Fuck you. Call yourself."

I slammed the door behind me and we sped off.

"Inside you are two wolves, one of rage, one of love," Kofi said. "You know which one wins?"

My hands shook. Adrenaline coursed through my veins. "Tell me."

"The one you feed."

"Let's get you back," I said.

Chapter 14

Mr. Ricci knocked on the door while I hung back. A short man in a suit answered. He had slicked back hair, with the stench of corporate asshole written all over him.

"Who are you?" he asked.

"I'm Mr. Ricci." He pointed to me. "This is my associate. We have a matter to discuss."

"I'm sorry, I'm late for—"

Mr. Ricci jammed a gun in his ribs. "I'm not asking."

The three of us took a seat at his oak table. The man brought us coffee.

Mr. Ricci was about to light up when the man objected. "Sir, no smoking. My wife—"

He lit. "Shut the fuck up. My associate here says Kleopatria was here."

The man shivered, taking a seat. "Yeah, about a week ago. Why?"

"She's dead."

"I didn't kill her."

"Listen guy," I said, "when she left she was white as a fuckin' ghost. She wasn't right."

"Well of course not."

"Of course not?" Mr. Ricci asked.

"Well no. Not with a medical procedure."

"The fuck you talkin' 'bout?" I asked.

"Wait," he said, "you cops?"

"We look like cops?" Mr. Ricci took a drag and drink of coffee. "What medical procedure?"

"Listen guys, I shouldn't be talkin'."

"Ok." Mr. Ricci gestured to me.

Fuck. I knew what I had to do.

I backhanded him. Blood dripped from his lip.

"Christ man," he said. "Relax."

"Spill the beans," I said, raising my hand again.

"Sometimes I do favors."

"Favors?" Mr. Ricci asked.

"Yeah," he said, wiping blood from his lip. "Women get pregnant and don't want to be."

"I'm curious." He paused, "Wait, we didn't get your name."

"Frank Black."

"I'm curious, Mr. Black. You don't strike me as a doctor."

"I have medical training." He paused. "I dropped out of medical school."

I hovered over him, like a viper ready to strike.

"See," Mr. Ricci said, "We have a problem. I had over $12,000 invested in her."

"Yeah," he said, "she told me something about Hollywood. She didn't seem keen on going."

"That's not relevant. What is relevant is I'm almost 12 large in the hole."

Frank shrugged. "Sorry mister."

"I don't quite think you know who I am." He took a sip of coffee. "You know Carlo Gambino?"

"Oh shit."

"Oh shit is right," Mr. Ricci said, cracking his knuckles. "I want my fuckin' money."

***

The afternoon turned to evening, and we left with only blood on our hands, and a body in the truck we later dumped in the river.

We leaned against the bridge and Mr. Ricci slipped me another envelope. "You did good."

"This don't feel good."

"We're going to get in my car, and this never happened."

"Ok."

"We never met. Someone asks about me, what do you say?"

"I keep my mouth shut."

He patted me on the head. "Good. Let's go."

***

He dropped me off at the bar, and I headed home. Blood stained my hands and I needed a shower. I assumed I was a simple driver for escorts, which is illegal enough. I entered my apartment, stripped off, and tears flowed in the shower.

"I'm trying to do right, Maria. I'm trying!"

I dried off and Henry called.

"Ricky," he said. "I've been callin' all fuckin' day."

"I was out. What is it?"

"We need to talk. Bring your ass down here in 30."

I hung up.

Oh, we need to talk alright. Maybe a strong conversation.

***

This was my only bump in with the mob, through my work with Esmerelda, she sang the praises of Carlo Gambino. She claimed he was a close friend, but I never saw him. She also said Carlo had a way of dealing with members who killed normal people.

"The Italians kill one another," she said. "Mr. Ricci? That fuckin' degenerate. Word has he started killin' regular motherfuckers shortly after Gambino made him in 1963." She paused. "Ricci was also selling cocaine on the side."

"So?"

"That's a death sentence. Gambino told me any member caught using, or dealing drugs was killed." She motioned the bartender to bring another martini. "Don't worry, I smoothed things over. You're clean. My advice? Don't fuck around with the Italians."

I nodded.

"You're a good man, Mr. Malone. Kofi was pretty shaken up." She took a drink. "The guy you beat? Well, let's just say word's spreading."

"Spreading?"

"You fuck around, and Mr. Malone smacks you the fuck down." She smirked. "What are your plans after all this?"

"Plans?"

"When you're done with parole and all that shit?"

"I just want to be free. Really free."

She laughed. "Don't we all?"

"I'm serious."

"Money buy's freedom, yeah? How long you got?"

"Till 1976."

"Then what?"

"California." I paused. "Open up a beachfront bar or something."

She extended her hand and I shook it. "Stick with me, Mr. Malone. When you make it to Cali, I expect a postcard."

I smiled. "Of course."

Chapter 15

"What do you think about utopianism?" Elizabeth asked.

"Ain't no such thing," I said.

"I think of it differently," she said. "Check this. We have the world, right? We see all the problems. The crime. The corruption. The poverty. The list goes on and on, right?"

"Yeah."

She smiled. "I think utopia is more a state of mind, ya know? Like, imaging the world could and should be better."

Such optimism rang a numb resonance. A better world? I just don't know.

"You don't believe me, huh?"

"No." I paused. "But I want to."

"Here," she said, "let me prove it. Imagine living in Mississippi in the 1800s. Who, but the bravest of souls, could have imagined a world where the negro wasn't in bondage?"

From everything I've seen, not much has changed except the chains. At the end of the day, what's the difference between living in fear of a master's whip, or a cop's fist? In prison I read The Constitution. The 13th Amendment makes slavery legal as punishment for crimes. The more things change, the more they stay the same.

"Or," she continued, "who could have imagined women voting?"

"I dunno," I said. "Your light shines brighter than mine."

I checked my watch and realized. Fuck. We were an hour ahead of schedule.

"I have to believe there's a light out there. Somewhere. No matter how faint."

"We have time to kill," I said. "My bad, I picked you up an hour early. You hungry?"

She rubbed her crucifix. "A little, I guess. More nervous."

"There's a diner a few miles ahead."

"Rick, I don't have money."

"It's on me."

She teared up. "You'd buy me a meal?"

"Sure, why not?"

She wiped her tears. "Nothing. Just…" She trailed off letting the car breathe silently. "Thank you."

I flashed a smile in the rearview. "I like pie, do you like pie?"

"I love pie."

I smiled. "Good."

***

We rolled up to Roxie's Golden Spoon. The last few months I'd come to know the place well. Roxie even let me wait at the booth by the phone, far enough from the Motown Jukebox to read the newspaper in peace, but close enough for tunes to roll over me.

We entered, The Supremes playing, a few kids danced and took a seat at my favorite booth. And to think, this was the last time. The sizzling burgers, the creamy milkshakes, and coffee only Roxie knew how to brew.

"Rick," Nancy said. "We just can't get rid of ya, eh? Who's the young lady?"

"I'm Elizabeth."

She leaned in and handed her a menu. "That's a gorgeous crucifix."

"Thanks."

"Regular, Rick?"

"Start me off with coffee," I said. "I'll decide when Elizabeth orders."

Should my last meal be a burger and fries? Dozens of times I've ordered that. Maria's favorite was chop steak with mashed potatoes, and green beans. We had that the night before she started treatment.

"Order anything, Elizabeth."

"I've never had a burger and fries."

"Never, sweetie?" Nancy asked. "We should change that." She grinned. "I bet you want a strawberry milkshake, don't you?"

She kept staring at the prices.

I clutched her hand. "Don't worry about it."

"Ok, yeah, that." She looked at Nancy's name tag. "Yeah, that all sounds swell."

"Regular, Rick?"

"Not today."

"Really? You always get the burger and fries."

"Roxie's Special," I said.

"Livin' dangerously, eh? Good for you. Be right up."

"Why are you so nice to me?" Elizabeth asked when Nancy departed.

I stared out the window at cars passing a homeless man. "There ain't enough kindness in the world." I checked my pack. Half gone. Barely enough to get me to the end. I lit up and took a drag. "Sometimes this world seems to only breed hatred and violence."

"Can I help you not to hurt?"

"Don't worry 'bout me. I'll be alright." If only that were true. "Let's just get you a nice meal."

***

I'd almost forgotten about my leg until it became engulfed in flame and could hardly shift in my seat.

"You ok?" she asked.

I took a sip of coffee. "My leg."

"Like before?"

I nodded, my hands shook, lighting a cigarette. "Distract me."

"Pardon?"

"Tell me about you."

"Like what?"

"Just…" My hands shook ash on the table. "Just…your story."

"It's not pleasant."

"They rarely are." The needles taunted me from the parking lot. "Please?"

She raised an eyebrow. "Ok."

Part Two: Elizabeth

Chapter 16

My first memory is witnessing my father kick my mother down the stairs. This became a regular thing, as did the hospital visits. The first time, I remember, she broke her arm. We lived out in the country, before my father inherited money, and the closet person was a young negro boy named Jimmy.

At the time, I didn't know why I hated my house. I just knew I didn't want to be there. Jimmy and I would run through the woods, and we found an abandoned cabin we claimed as our castle.

"What do you want to be when you're big?" I asked.

"A doctor." He hung his head. "My parents said that's not possible."

"Why?"

He pointed to his skin.

"I don't understand."

He shrugged. "Maybe Captain America! Punching bad people in the kisser! Yeah! Like Superman did to Hitler in the comics!"

We laughed and ran around our castle. My dad said to be home before supper, but he was too drunk to notice if I came or went. Jimmy and I would lay out in the evening dew and look up at the flickering sky.

"Do you believe in aliens?" he asked.

"I dunno." I paused, soaking in the tapestry above. "The recent Roswell incident is interesting though."

"My pops thinks it's a conspiracy," Jimmy said. "He thinks everything is."

"Conspiracy?"

"I don't think he's well."

"I'm sorry," I said.

"I do." Jimmy paused. "Believe in aliens, that is. And I believe they are different from us. I believe they're kind. That they're watching us. Like in Twilight Zone episodes."

Jimmy was my world for the summer of 61.

We got older, and his face started sinking by the summer of 63. He became less of my world.

By 64, I hardly recognized him. Something changed, and at the time, I didn't know what. Neither of us talked about our families much. We preferred to live in the world we created just for us. But Jimmy moved with defeat, as if he were carrying a boulder. As if the world scraped his bones against concrete.

"People hate me," he said, "and they don't even know me."

"How can you hate someone you don't know?"

He shrugged and pointed to his skin.

The last time we saw each other was August 18th, 1964. I hung by the abandoned cabin and he came over, shirt torn, and blood dripping from his nose. His eyes were like broken mirrors, as if nothing penetrated.

"Jimmy, who did this?"

"It's nothing," he said. "Can we just look at the stars?"

"Jimmy, this is serious."

"Please." A tear rolled down his cheek. "I just wanna look at the stars."

I put my arm around him. "Ok."

"I want you to know you were always super swell."

***

"Aren't the stars amazing?" We must have lain there for hours.

"They were." He got up and started leaving. "At one time they were magic."

"They still are, right?"

"Sure…"

"See you tomorrow?"

"Yeah, sure."

The next day Jimmy didn't show up as usual, so I wandered through the woods until I found him hanging from a tree, bleeding from the groin. I tried to cut him down, but he was too high up.

I never returned to the cabin. And until now, I never told anyone. But Jimmy was the best there was. With a smile, he could illuminate the sky. Over several years I saw a boy turn to an old man. Years later I found out a local KKK chapter hung him. You can probably guess why he bled from the groin.

And then I was alone until we moved into the city.

***

The waitress brought us our food. Hard to imagine someone living to their teens and not experiencing something as all-American as a burger and fries. I'd smelled em before.

But despite my family being rich on paper, Dad refused to spend a nickel he didn't have to. My mom chalked it up to him living through the depression as a boy.

"So the KKK got to Jimmy?" Rick asked.

"So I heard," I said, popping a fry into my mouth. "On good days, I'd like to think he decided to check out. I know that sounds morbid. But it sound's less horrific than a lynching."

Rick watched the steak, as though trying to divine something from it. Someone once said there are people broken beyond repair. I never bought into that. But there was something about Rick that made me think his spirit left long ago. Maybe I just wanted to make him not hurt for a little bit.

He cut into his steak and took a bite. "Ok, can I hear more?"

***

The house we moved to is where you picked me up. The neighborhood is nice enough, I suppose, but I miss the forest. In place of the forest, I'd spend my days in the library, even after my dad quit drinking. He tried bonding with me, but why? Sometimes it's too late to atone.

There's something about families never talked about. We always hear about the abusive ones, or the ones that resemble a Norman Rockwell painting. What we never hear about is the mainline indifference that radiates from so many. The wanton indifference. The absence of affection. They say Mother and Father are God to children. They were just strangers to me.

My dad never hurt me. My mom never hurt me. My relatives never hurt me. But they left a void. Looking at my family is like looking at a stranger's painting. Would I feel bad if Dad died? I don't think I'd feel anything. They never said they loved me.

When my aunt died, they drug me to the funeral. People told stories about how great she was. They waxed on and on and I didn't understand. I'd seen her many times, but never spoken with her at length. I don't think she knew my name.

When at the funeral, I thought: I should feel something. It wasn't until years later I realized: I don't feel much for the homicides in the newspapers. And at the end of the day, my aunt was just someone in a newspaper. A stranger who happened to be related to me.

I suppose family means more to some than others.

***

"In my experience," Rick said, "family is overrated. Patriotism too."

"Not a flag waver?"

"When I was homeless, I saw a fair number of World War II vets." He paused, taking another bite of steak. "These men fought to end fascism. And they were homeless." He paused to chew. "Heard of Alan Turing?"

"No."

"Brilliant mathematician. Cracked Nazi codes. Without him, who knows what Hitler would have done." Rick lit a cigarette and stared out the window. "The Brits convicted him of indecency for being a queer. The poor bastard killed himself for what the British government did to him." He took a sip of coffee. "No, I'm not much on waving flags."

"You sound like Billy."

"Billy?"

***

Billy was what you might call my first crush. Maybe my first love, even though I was only 12 or 13. At school I'd watch him. He seemed like he had the world at his fingertips. He didn't fit in and didn't care much.

One day he approached me. "I see you watching me."

"Oh," I said, "sorry."

"Don't be. Hey, listen, this school sucks, yeah?"

"I suppose."

He pointed to the jocks. "Look at them. They're goin' nowhere in life. You can count on that. In 20 years, they'll be here flipping burgers drowning their lives with wives they hate and children who end up in prison." He sat next to me. "So what's your deal? You're always alone."

"So are you."

"Yeah, but I kind of hate people. Especially the rich pricks here. These assholes are bad for my health. Want to, I dunno, just skip the rest of the day?"

"And do what?"

"Heard of Paul Newman?"

"No."

"Really? Damn," he said. "Look, this cat can act. He's in a new film: Cool Hand Luke. I've seen it before, and this dude don't take shit from nobody. You might like it. And I want to be just like Luke. You in?"

Besides Jimmy, nobody really ever took an interest in me. Why not, right? We went, and I think he enjoyed the film more than I did. But it was fine. We got milkshakes after. And he kissed me.

One day he came to school with a busted lip and black eye.

"What happened?" I asked.

"It's nothing."

One day he came to school with a cast on his arm. Same thing: It's nothing.

Then one day he never came back, and his father went to prison.

***

"The old man beat him to death?" Rick said, finishing the meal. "My old man was a real son of a bitch too."

"I really liked Billy. We had a few good months. He taught me people do care." I paused, wiping a tear from my cheek. "At least sometimes."

"Sometimes," Rick said. "Sometimes."

"That's about all I care to remember from childhood." I paused, trying not to cry. "It got worse in high school."

Chapter 17

Girls never liked me in school. Sometimes I'd see women with picket signs or handing out fliers. They said they were feminists. Being a young girl, I didn't know what they were talking about. I didn't know what got them all riled up. But I did assume a kind of sisterly love and I assumed with age came female companionship.

When entering high school, I learned there wasn't any such thing. I'd see the black girls fighting the white girls, and the preppy white girls do everything to backstab other preppy girls. None of it made sense. It still doesn't.

My first day I sat alone at a lunch table, the other girls whispering, the jocks doing whatever they do, and everyone else mostly ignoring me. Alone again, the shadow that hung from my neck. But this time it didn't bother me.

"Hey, ok if I sit?" the girl asked.

I shrugged. "Free country."

"Yeah," she said, "so they say. I'm Ezra."

"I'm Elizabeth."

"Well," Ezra said, "hope you don't mind sitting by a Jew."

"Why would I?"

She laughed. "Good. You're not like the rest of these motherfuckers. They all assume I'm some Shylock."

"From Shakespeare?"

"Well I'll be goddamned, girl. You actually know shit."

I shrugged. "I've spent time in libraries."

She laughed. "Keep that to yourself. It's dangerous to be too smart in this country." She paused. "Know what they did to black people who could read?"

"No."

Ezra made the noose hanging gesture. "That's what happened."

"With all due respect," I said, "you don't sound like I imagined a Jew to sound?"

"Like, all religious and holy?"

I nodded.

She laughed. "Not that kind of Jew. Had a ham sandwich the other day." She paused. "At least I don't have to suffer boring-ass temple."

"My parents are Catholic. Well, on paper."

"You?"

"Don't really give it much thought. I suppose. Sure?"

She winked. "Yeah, religion is dead people's baggage as I see it."

A boy in a football jersey passed us. "Kike."

Another passed. "Whore."

"Hey Mike," she said, "saw your faggot dad suckin' a dude off. Go fuck yerself after you fuck yer good for nothing mother."

"Gonna let some fuckin' Jew bitch talk to you that way, Mike?" someone chimed in.

"Hey," Principal Montgomery said. "Enough. Ezra, watch your mouth." He grabbed Mike by the ear. "Come with me. We've talked about this."

The lunchroom fell quiet.

"You're not scared of Mike?"

"Nah," she said. "I've taken punches before. Mike knows it too."

"I like you," I said.

"You seem cool. Yeah, you're not some stuck up bitch." She pointed to a blonde in ponytails. "But she is. Fuck her."

***

Rick got a third cup of coffee and lit another cigarette. His eyes screamed something I couldn't put my finger on. Something beyond pain. Something beyond numbness, as if a force pulled him from a void of melancholy.

"You seem to get around," I said, "know any Jews?"

"Sure," he said.

"And?"

"I don't know much, but I know any group of people with faith have shades of gray." He took a drag. "I've met a lot of folks. Some good, most not so good."

"Ezra was good," I said. "Yeah...real good."

Rick finished his steak. "Go on."

***

Like all good things, they eventually end. We'd go for walks, but she refused to take me to her place. Maybe I hoped her family could be mine? Looking back on it, she never talked about her parents much. When I'd bring it up, she'd change the subject.

"I'm not here for a long time," she'd say, "just a good time."

At the time, I didn't know what that meant until one day she had to use crutches. She refused to talk about it. After a month or so the cast came off, but sometimes I'd catch a glimpse of scars. One on her neck. And when she bent over, her shirt came up and I saw burn marks.

And I knew. And I also knew she wouldn't talk about it. And I knew soon I'd be alone again.

"Life is funny, ya know?" she said as we laid in the grass watching the clouds. "We're here for a blink and then gone, ya know?"

"Can we talk?"

"We are."

"No," I said. "I mean…"

"I got something better. Check this." She started laughing. "You'll like this joke. I stole it from Rusty Warren. Heard of her?"

"No."

"Yeah, most haven't. The prudes hate her. They squawk like chickens about her humor robbing sex of sophistication and whatnot. But she's great."

"What's the joke?"

"Ok," she tried holding back laughter.

She sang me the lyrics to Bounce Your Boobies and The Knockers Up Gal. I never laughed so hard and couldn't believe such songs existed.

"Did they air these on the radio?"

Ezra laughed even harder. "You kidding? Of course not."

Time spent with Ezra made time disappear. She made me feel good about being me. And almost every day she had some new joke. And some new wound. Sometimes she'd bring a bottle of alcohol and offer me some. I didn't like the taste.

"Life's a hell of a thing, Lizzy," she said, half drunk, as we laid in the grass.

"I love you," I said, blushing. "Not like that. Like. Oh hell."

She burst out laughing and put her arm around me. "I feel ya. Mutual."

Last time I saw her was before Christmas break my freshman year. We hid behind trees and belted random people with snowballs before running off to hide.

"Well," she said, "I better get home."

I smiled. "I'll miss you. See you in a few weeks."

She looked at me with a sense of calm. "I'm glad I knew you."

I didn't pick up on the past tense. All the signs I'd ignored over the months.

I saw her skip down the sidewalk.

And that was that.

***

I started tearing up and Rick handed me a napkin.

"Sorry," I said.

"It's ok."

"What happened?"

"Her father had a darkness to him."

Rick took a long drag. "Yeah. Mine too."

"He…" I tried holding back tears. "He touched her."

Rick hung his head. "I'm sorry."

"One day he touched her too much. And she snapped. She ummm, well, let's just say her bathwater was red."

Rick nodded.

"It only gets worse from there."

"Listen Elizabeth," he said, "I'm not judging. I'm a long-time actor in the theater of pain."

"Ok."

***

I went to her grave with a bottle of stolen Jack Daniels in the spring. Birds chirped, and the cemetery was empty.

Ezra Anna Goldmann

June 2nd 1955 - December 27th 1971

A shining star, burning bright in our hearts

Word was, her mother had no idea. She had no brothers or sisters, just like me. I did hear that shortly after Ezra's death, they got a divorce. I think her dad moved to Florida, but her mom is still around here somewhere.

I filled the second half of freshman year with booze. I'd skip class and drink under the bleachers. Or I'd fall asleep by Ezra's grave, only to wake up with a hangover.

I realized what Ezra meant when she'd say: I'm not here for a long time, just a good time. Maybe it started as a joke, something edgy, but I think she finally realized some of us don't make it far in this life.

Somewhere, deep inside, she knew she'd never make it to 18. The sense of peace when she said goodbye still haunts me. As if she'd given up and, in a way, was free. I wish I could have done something to make her hold on.

My grades started slipping, and I started losing time. When summer rolled around, I'd stopped going to the library.

Sophomore year rolled around, and the worst of it came.

Chapter 18

Until my sophomore year in high school, I can't think of anything I aspired to be. I suppose I was just surviving one day at a time. Sure, I'd dream of riding unicorns or fighting sea monsters as a little girl, but beyond that? I guess I never really thought much about the future. Girls like me exist in a futureless future.

The other girls in school yammered on and on about being a housewife and snagging a rich husband. Others had Hollywood dreams, others singing dreams. It wasn't until Mr. Larson lit a fire inside me for mathematics that I started dreaming again.

"William Playfair invented charts," he opened on the first day of class. "James Maxwell invented color pictures. Blaise Pascal invented the first calculator. What do all these men have in common?" He paused and nobody responded. "They were mathematicians."

I raised my hand. "Didn't Isaac Newton invent Calculus?"

He cocked his head. "Very good. Though a man named Leibniz would argue differently."

"Mathematicians ended the war," he continued. "Mathematicians drink from the fountain of the gods."

The other students looked at him as if he were crazy. How could someone get so excited about something we'd all considered boring? There was a life to Mr. Larson when he spoke about mathematics. I was sold the first day. I wanted to become a mathematician and save the world.

I devoted those first few months to his geometry course. Other classes be damned. I was getting average marks in other classes, but I aced every geometry exam. And he really liked me, too. By the time Christmas rolled around, I ended with a bunch of C's and an A in Geometry.

"You're built for mathematics," he said after class before Christmas break. "I've been doing this for almost 20 years, and you're one of only three people who walked out of here with an A." He paused. "Do you want a career in mathematics?"

"Yes."

"Then you need to go to college, and possibly graduate school."

"Ok?"

"And to do that," he said, "you have to get your grades up for your other courses."

"Oh…"

"You have time," he said. "Here's the deal. I'm one of the only teachers here with a master's degree in mathematics. I did my work at Berkeley.

"Where's that?" I asked.

"California," he said. "Do me a favor?"

"What?"

"By the start of senior year, get your GPA up to a 3.5, and I'll pull strings at Berkeley." He paused. "I can't guarantee anything, but my word carries some water."

I nodded. "Yes sir. 3.5."

"I believe in you, ok? You need to believe in you."

I smiled, then cried. "Thank you."

"Thank me when you win Field's Medal."

He was the first adult I thought cared about me.

***

Rick snuffed out his cigarette, but never took his eyes off me.

"Elizabeth," he said, "I need to use the restroom quickly."

"Ok."

"Refill?" Nancy asked.

"One more, then we have to leave."

"Sure thing, hun."

"Sweetie," she turned towards me. "You hardly touched the milkshake."

I cracked a grin. "I'm savoring it."

"Rick," Nancy pointed to the milkshake once Rick returned. "She's savoring it. You guys can learn from us gals."

"Alright, alright, Nancy."

"You be good now," Nancy said, sliding the bill to him. "Whenever you're ready."

He nodded.

"She seems nice," I said.

"She's fine," he said, lighting up another cigarette. "Mathematician, eh?"

"What?"

"Your dream." He took a drag. "I was downright terrible at math. Kudos to you though."

"Dream…" I trailed off. "Yeah, dream."

"Not anymore?" Rick asked.

Silence rang across the booth.

"Sorry, did I—"

"You sure you want to hear more?"

Rick checked his watch and nodded.

***

During Christmas break, I got three books from the library. Euclid's Elements, George Boole's The Laws of Thought, and Abram Wald's Statistical Decision Functions. Beyond Euclid, I admit the other two were over my head. I didn't understand most of it, but there was a beauty in the equations and proofs.

I felt alive. I hadn't felt this alive since my time with Jimmy staring up at the night sky. Mom and dad didn't know what to make of the whole ordeal. My dad was convinced I'd never be a mathematician. In his mind, women were incapable of mathematics. From what little he spoke to me, he thought I just needed a husband. My mother was equally perplexed. I wasn't interested in boys (well, not too much). I even attempted to surprise them by proving Cantor's theorem that there are higher order infinities (something Mr. Larson showed me one day after school). *That's nice, dear or I don't get the big deal, were the responses.*

***

"Rick," I said, "I can show you Cantor's theorem if you wish."

"I'd love to see it," he said, "but I'm afraid it'd be over my head."

"Oh…"

"No, it's not that I'm not interested. It's…"

"It's ok."

"Listen, Elizabeth. I dropped out of high school. I know cars. That's about it."

"That's it?"

Ricked rubbed his knuckle bandages. "I know other things. But not mathematics."

"Trust me on this then. Mathematical space is vaster than the known universe."

Rick cracked a grin. "I have no doubt."

***

Christmas break ended, and I couldn't wait to get back to school. I got to pick an elective, and while most people chose theater or something like that, I picked Mr. Larson's advanced geometry course. Before break, he told me by the end of the course, we'd prove the independence of Euclid's parallel postulate, which opened up a whole new area of mathematics: non-Euclidean geometry.

When my first report card came out, I managed a few Bs in my other courses. I rushed to show Mr. Larson and he patted me on the back.

"Well done," he said.

"I'm aiming for all A's Junior year."

"I see you're struggling a bit with World History and American Literature." He paused. "I'm no expert in either, but want to come by my place in the evenings and I can help?"

"Really? No foolin'?"

"No foolin'." He smiled.

The other teachers thought of me as a girl. I thought Mr. Larson thought of me as a person. Nobody else said I could do anything but be a housewife. As it turns out, Mr. Larson had a mask.

***

"We should probably hit the road," Rick said, downing the last cup and putting a $50 on the table.

"That's a lot," I said.

"Nancy needs it more than I do," he said. "Especially now. Let's go."

"You got a big heart."

"I dunno," he said, "continue the story on the road?"

"Ok."

Chapter 19

We got out of the parking lot and Rick motioned for me to ride shotgun. I slumped down in the seat and we headed down the road.

"Mind if I have one of your cigarettes?" I asked.

"Didn't know you smoked."

"I usually don't," I said. "But this next part I need one."

"You don't have to tell me," he said, lighting a cigarette and passing it to me. "If it's too—"

"I need to." I took a drag. "Promise to believe me?"

"I know where this is going. Hit me."

I took another drag. "Ok."

***

The first weeks Mr. Larson acted normal. His wife was there, and she'd offer cookies and iced tea. Sometimes she'd sit down and help with my homework. Mr. Larson said she devoured classic literature, so he'd sometimes rely on her for English homework.

The end of the third week, they invited me over for dinner. Mrs. Larson made a delicious pot roast with potatoes and carrots. We rounded off the dinner with peach pie.

"Darling," Mrs. Larson said, "I must say, of the student's my husband's tutored, you just might be the brightest."

"I have a good eye," he said. "I know talent when I see it."

"I really appreciate all you do," I said. "Thank you."

"Our pleasure," she said. "Why mathematics?"

"It's the cream of the gods," I said.

"Dear lord," she rolled her eyes. "He's rubbing off on you."

Mr. Larson laughed. "Cream of the gods, darling. Cream of—"

"The gods. Yes, yes," she said walking away.

"It'll click someday." He winked at me.

"I just don't get the appeal." She returned with a cigarette in hand.

"There's just something…" I trailed off, unsure what to say. "I dunno. Elegant. Beautiful. It can be so pure. Mathematics doesn't judge."

Mr. Larson clapped. "See? She gets it."

"Alright, alright. Fine. I'm off to do dishes."

He leaned in. "You and I get it. Not everyone does. That's what makes you special."

***

I'd look over at Rick and couldn't help seeing Jimmy during his final days. Some people have a way about them. A way where life's given them too many raw deals, with too many doors shut, and the only windows they fell through left them covered in glass.

"You sure you're ok?" I asked.

Rick lit a cigarette. "I'm fine."

"Your bandages don't look fine." I can't believe I'm just now noticing.

"Sometimes I punch walls."

I don't know why I clicked with Rick. Maybe it's because we both bleed pain. Or maybe it's because we've lived life too fast, and too hard. I feel 40. I can't imagine how old Rick feels.

I took another drag and flicked the butt out the window. "Is it ok if I have another?"

"Sure."

"This next part…" I trailed off. "Nobody believes this next part."

"Life ain't Leave it to Beaver," Rick said. "Hit me."

***

Mr. Larson always wore a suit, even during tutoring. My running joke was he slept in the damn thing. One night I go over, and he's in a bathrobe holding a glass of auburn liquid. I think scotch?

"Sorry," he said, "I forgot we had a meeting."

"I can come back tomorrow."

"No, it's fine," he said, motioning me in. "Wife's out with her friends doing women stuff or something."

All the signs were there. Everything in me said: run. Just get the fuck outta there. But I was getting more Bs in classes. A few A's too. I really wish I'd never gone in.

"You sure?" I asked.

"Of course." He grabbed my hand and brought me inside.

He led me to the couch, not our normal spot at the kitchen table.

"Why the couch?" I asked.

"Bad back. It acts up."

"You know you're special, right?"

I didn't know what to say.

"And beautiful. One of the most beautiful women I know. Yes, a woman. Not a girl." He set his hand on my thigh. "I've helped you out, right?"

I froze.

"Right?"

"More than you know."

"Nothing in this world's free." He opened his robe revealing his erection. "Help me out."

It started off with blowjobs when his wife was out. After the first night, I walked home, unsure of what happened. I do know I brushed my teeth several times, and cried in the bathtub, and didn't know why.

"This is between us, ok?" he said.

I nodded.

"I talked to the teachers," he said, "Not a single C. All Bs and As." He gazed into my eyes. "Want to keep it that way?"

I nodded.

"Good." He started untying his robe.

**

Rick pulled over and exited the car. I watched him watch the cars as he smoked. I saw his arms twitch, and his hands ball up. Then he returned.

"Sorry," he said.

"It's ok. I can stop."

"I need you to go on."

"Why?"

"My wife," he said, "had the same teacher."

"Really?"

"Unless it's a different Mr. Larson." We started on the road again. "Go on. Please."

***

Time went on and he wanted more than blowjobs. You can fill in the rest. If you know Mr. Larson, you know he comes from money. And as the old saying goes: money talks, bullshit walks.

I missed a period. I started vomiting. And I knew I was pregnant. I just wanted to be a mathematician. I wanted to find a husband someday. And I wanted to be something. Make something of myself.

I tried hiding the whole ordeal, but eventually I began showing.

"My wife said he was in his late 20s when she had him," Rick said. "Was he older?"

"Sure," I said. "Grey hair, receding hairline. Prob 50s."

Rick stared down the road. Blood soaking through his bandages. Was he white knuckling the steering wheel?

"I shouldn't put this on you, Rick."

"He still alive?"

"As far as I know."

"Elizabeth, you may not think it, but I'm a bad man." He paused. "I asked my wife where he lived, but she never told me."

His knuckle bandages revealed more of what I already knew. Rick knew more than just cars. He knew how to hurt people. He didn't punch walls. He cracked bones.

"What are you asking me?"

"I can hurt him if you want." He took a drag. "But I need your permission."

"Aren't we going to be late?"

"I'll take care of it."

"You really want to hurt him, don't you?"

"The only real justice is found in the streets." His face scowled. "Civilized man fancies himself a man of laws. Of justice." Blood soaked through his bandages. "There's only the law of the jungle."

He pulled over at a gas station and went to a payphone. He seemed to be there for hours, but I bet it was only a few minutes.

"I bought us thirty minutes," he said.

I told him the address. "You're sure?"

"Yes," he said.

"Can I watch?"

"No. You don't want nightmares."

Chapter 20

Everything moved pretty quickly after I told my parents. My mother wanted to send me to a convent, some place for girls to have children and then be put up for adoption. My father had gained stature in the community, and said he knew a guy who knew a guy, and got a phone number for a man who could make the problem go away easier.

The way my father understood it, keeping up a lie for months was too hard. How long can a girl be on vacation? I found out my father was more interested in making problems go away than solving them.

The morning before I met you, I returned all my mathematics books. A dream had been tainted. The purity of mathematics was now painted with a brush of pain. As I walked back home, I realized I was more than alone.

I was disposable.

I was nothing more than a problem.

I was suckered into believing I could be seen as anything but a girl, or woman.

My remaining days were spent in my room, staring out the window dreaming. I'd mapped out my whole life. Until today, I imagined I'd be in a large lecture hall, writing equations on the board, showing students the beauty of mathematics. I allowed myself to imagine I'd work with other mathematicians to make major breakthroughs. And I imagined my office, filled with exams to grade.

Staring out the window, those images took on a shade of gray. Would the other professors hire me? If they did hire me, would they just use me as a sex object? Would I ever be one of them, or just an outsider looking in, shivering in the cold?

As the hours ticked by, I waited for someone to comfort me. Maybe, just maybe, my mom or dad would show some kindness to me.

My door opened.

"He's here," my father said, "don't keep him waiting."

***

Rick drove fast but handled the car with ease. The engine sang, and his face had a coldness to it. Not a stoic resignation, a kind of refined sociopathy. The kind you turn on and off with a switch. One minute he's comforting a crying woman, the next, breaking someone's nose before returning to a woman's warm embrace.

"Rick, I—"

He held up his hand. "Tell me after."

I looked in the passenger side mirror. A black car was following us.

"A car's following us," I blurted out.

"I know. Please, I need you to be silent."

Part Three: Rick

Chapter 21

Before we left the diner, I had a run in with a certain detective.

"Elizabeth," I said, "I need to use the restroom quickly."

"Ok."

While pissing in the stall a man stood beside me. "I know what you are."

"Good for you, pal."

"You won't get away with it."

"I'm sure I won't."

"See," the man said, "I'm Detective McKinny."

"Good for fuckin' you."

"Listen you piece of white trash," he said, "when I get the evidence, I'm—"

"Am I under arrest?" I zipped my fly.

"No."

"Good." I headed for the door.

"Hey, I'm not done—"

"Listen detective." I leaned in, "we're alone in here. Be a damn shame if your head broke the mirror."

"Threatening an officer, are we?"

"Not at all. Just saying it'd be a shame."

"Let's talk outside," he said.

"Nah, let's not." I headed for the door again.

"I'll be seeing you real soon, Mr. Malone."

"Not in this lifetime."

***

I parked outside Mark's house. The black car stopped too.

"Can you do me a favor?" I asked.

Elizabeth clutched her crucifix. "Ok?"

"There's going to be ugliness." I turned on the radio playing Led Zeppelin's Heartbreaker. "I want you to listen to the radio and stay in the car."

"I'm a bit scared."

"I know. Just focus on the music." I turned up the volume.

I hobbled over to the black car. Detective McKinny. He rolled down the window.

"Rick," he said, "just keeping—"

I placed my pistol to his temple. "Let's walk."

If memory serves, there's a river close to this area.

"You shoot me, you'll have every fuckin' cop on your fuckin' ass."

"Maybe," I said, "and maybe I'm so goddamn crazy I don't give a fuck. Wanna roll those dice, cowboy?"

He glared at me.

"Get the fuck outta the fuckin' car, gumshoe."

We strolled down a path, passed the houses, and into a wooded area.

"You won't get away with this, you fuckin' mick."

"I don't expect to."

"We both know how this is gonna end," he said. "Do me a favor and at least admit to what you all did."

I pistol whipped him and his head cranked to the side. Blood poured out his mouth.

"Shut the fuck up."

We reached the river.

"Mr. Malone," he choked out through the blood. "I have a family."

You don't rise to his rank without taking many envelopes.

"Please. I'm—"

I took out my knife and slit him ear to ear, then kicked him in the river. I went back to my trunk and grabbed a fresh shirt.

Elizabeth seemed oblivious. Good.

I rapped on Mark's door.

"Can I help you?"

"Mark Larson?"

"And you are?"

I shoved the gun in his face. "You alone?"

"Wife's out."

I pushed my way inside.

"What's this about?" he asked.

"Let's chat."

***

I kept my gun at Mark as we moved to his oak table and sat down. "You were a new teacher when Maria attended?"

"Who?"

"I will pistol whip the fuck outta you."

"Yeah, sure, I guess."

I set a knife on the table and grabbed his hand. "How many girls?"

"I'm sorry," he started crying. "I don't know what sickness is in me."

I put the knife to his pinky. "How many?"

"Over a dozen."

"Why Maria? Why Elizabeth?"

He glared at me. "In every group there's a weak link. They were the weak links for predators like me."

I nodded.

"What was Maria like?"

"It's been a long—"

I dug the knife into the joint and he howled. "Nice...Sweet."

"You were the reason she cut ties with her family, weren't you?"

"I know nothing about that," he choked out.

"Maria was a wonderful woman," I said. "An angel."

"What's she to you?"

"She was my wife."

"Oh shit."

I nodded. "Yeah. Was. Past tense."

"I don't suppose I'll make it out alive?"

I took the knife and positioned myself behind him. "I've wanted to kill you for over 20 years."

Blood sprayed on the table and his eyes grew cold as I watched him bleed out.

**

"Any good tunes?" I asked, returning to the car, shoving the knife in the glove compartment.

"Pretty wild ones," Elizabeth said.

"I'm told it's what the kids like." I started the car and headed down the road. "I'm more of a jazz man."

"Elizabeth looked back. "The black car isn't moving."

"And it won't."

"Did you see anything? Hear anything?"

"No."

"Elizabeth," I said, "You think I have a good heart." Long pause.

"Go on."

"I don't. There's a darkness."

"That's just the outer shell," she said, "underneath is something good."

"I dunno."

"You're the only person who ever seemed to care. About me. To ask about me."

I lit a cigarette. I had four remaining. "Let's get you to the clinic."

Chapter 22

I barged into Henry's office and threw the obituary of Kleopatria on his desk.

"Did I call you?" he said.

"Tell me what kind of driver I am."

"You're getting paid, what do you care?"

"Well," I said, "I assumed I was driving high class escorts. Apparently, that's not the case. I know what kind of driver I am. I want you to say it."

"You got a wire or something? Go fuck yerself."

I lifted up my shirt. "I drive women to get abortions, don't I?"

He nodded.

"This a lucrative business?"

"It can be." He poured himself a bourdon. "People like husher-uppers. That's what we are."

"The fuck's that mean?"

"It means we're paid not to know. Not to talk. To keep legitimate people legitimate."

"So that's what I do?"

"And escorts. Jack-of-all driving trades, Ricky boy."

"You're a real cocksucker, Henry. Pulling me into this shit."

"Listen pal, like it or not, I'm the best friend you got."

I stormed out.

***

After a few weeks on the street, I bumped into a pimp named DJ Sparkles who said in 1963 Henry got in on the numbers racket. The bosses got wind Henry skimmed too much from the top.

"Henry ain't smart, Malone," DJ Sparkles said. "Afta da bosses got hold'a his ass, that dumb motherfucka drank outta straws fer bout a year." He laughed licking his joint. "Dumb bitch tried shakin' me down few months back, ya feel? This fuckin' guy's always runnin' some grift."

"What happened?"

"He pissed his pants when ma gals smacked him about. Golden Shower Henry. Dat's his new name 'round here." He pulled out a knife. "Fucker shows his ass here again, I'll cut his fuckin' nuts off."

"So he's mob connected?"

"Not no mo. He's stupid as fuck, man." He lit the joint and the skunk smell pierced my nostrils. "He wanted to be a made guy," he laughed. "He's not even Italian. I'm tellin' ya, Rick. He's more worthless than a used condom."

DJ was always nice to me, and sometimes I'd do driving work for him. He paid well, and he was one of the few pimps who seemed to care for his girls (despite Esmerelda's insistence that he didn't).

"Wanna hear a prediction, Rick?" DJ asked.

"Ok."

"You like jazz, right?"

I nodded.

"I know some cats who are melding jazz with poetry. I call it spoken word Jazz. They do some weird shit with records. Like a scratching sound." He inhaled and coughed. "Sounds real nice."

"What's the prediction?"

"It'll take time, but I bet by the mid to late 80s, this new musical form will be bigger than Motown."

I shrugged. "Motown's pretty big."

"It might be a way for a lot of us to get off the street." He took a drag. "And seriously man, get the fuck away from Henry."

"Can't, he's my P.O."

He shook his head. "Always the dumbest assholes in charge, isn't it?"

I nodded.

Who knows if DJ's predictions will come true but I went to see him one day and his girls informed me he'd been killed. Shot in the back six times fleeing from police.

***

A few more months passed, and more elites started hitting up Henry. Oil men, politicians, diplomats, anyone on the right side of capitalism.

"You really want to know why they didn't bury him?" Howard McIntyre asked, puffing on a pre-Castro Cabana, sipping a glass of 1937 Glenfiddich, his yacht swaying back and forth.

I nodded.

"To send a message. Few years back, José Miguel Battle, the man himself, in the flesh, told me Henry's a billboard now." He puffed harder and my eyes began to water. "The Italians tell folks that too. Billboard Henry they call him."

"Mr. McIntyre, if I may ask another question?"

"Howard," he said. "You did my family right, by all means."

My scabbed knuckles itched. "If you'll excuse my language, many of girls end up reproductively fucked. Doesn't this—"

"Whores, Rick..." Mr. McIntyre poured himself another glass and offered one to me, but I declined. "It's not my daughter, or the daughters of my kind. It's hookers, pal. Many strung out and broken. Ya think anyone cares? The pimps? The police? The politicians?" He downed the scotch and poured himself another. "I know you ain't green, pal. Your eyes don't lie, nor your knuckles."

"With all due respect," I said, "these are human beings."

"Hey, listen, look, I got nothin' against prostitution. I've gotten my fair share of fellatio when the old bitch is off to do her little theater thing. It's an honorable profession if you ask me. With that said, besides you, and maybe some goodie goodie feminist types, ya think anyone really cares?"

"I suppose not."

"Listen Rick," Howard said, "As I said: you did my family right. And you know to only open your mouth at the dentist. You want to be a racecar driver?"

"Yes sir."

"I won't lie," he said, "pushin' middle age isn't kind to certain professions." He cracked a window and smoke poured out. "Finish up with Henry, then come see me." He slid me his business card. His face turned cold. "But get away from Henry when you can. He's a natural born loser."

I chuckled. "Don't I know it."

Howard checked his watch. "I got a meeting soon. Call me, ok?"

"Yes sir."

Chapter 23

I kept looking over at Elizabeth's crucifix. For people brutalized, marginalized, and beaten down, why do people think God cares? Is it instinct? Fear of mortality? If my father taught me anything after beating me in a drunken stupor, there's no cosmic justice. Nothing higher seems to give a damn. People always find Jesus when in the worst ways. They must perceive things differently than me.

"I see you eyeing the crucifix," Elizabeth said.

"Guilty as charged."

"You don't strike me as a religious man."

"Also guilty as charged." I paused. "May I ask a question?"

"Sure."

"Why?"

"Why what?"

"Why believe?"

She stared out the window. "I dunno. I'd like to think something out there cares."

"I see."

"Maybe I really don't believe, but just want to believe. There's this beautiful Cathedral. St. Thomas. I'd go there between masses and just sit. It felt nice."

"St. Thomas?"

"Yeah."

"My wife, her name was Maria. Well, she used to drag me there."

"Do you have a picture?"

I took a wedding photo out of my jacket and handed it to her. Her face turned white.

"What?"

"What was her maiden name?"

"Keller."

"My last name is Keller," she said. "I think this is my aunt."

"And you never met her?"

"No, just heard stories." She handed the picture back and I put it back in my jacket.

"So, she was your wife?"

"Yeah, was."

"I used to visit her grave."

"Leave notes?"

She smiled. "Yeah, I left dozens."

"I saw a few."

"How'd she die?" Elizabeth asked. "The family says she died on the streets as a hooker."

"I see."

"How'd she really pass?"

"She was my everything, Elizabeth." I paused, lighting a cigarette. "Officially, she died of cancer. But I think she died of a broken heart."

"I'm sorry, Rick."

"Yeah…"

"Ya think anyone gets over grief?"

"No," I said, "it just changes shape. You find some way to live with it."

"I wish I could have known her." She paused. "Rick, when this is all done, maybe someday we can visit her grave together?" She smiled. "Rick, can I ask something else?"

"Ok."

"Will you be my family?"

If only I'd not made so many bad decisions. It seems like my life is a series of decisions going from bad to worse. But this is my last ride in more ways than one.

"I'd like that very much."

She smiled.

"Don't ask me to help you with math homework."

She laughed. "I won't, but you'll teach me to drive?"

I kept tears locked inside. "Sure."

Chapter 24

Henry rang me after my first morning cup, and before my first good shit.

"Meet me in 30. Mickey's Tavern."

I checked my watch. 8:30AM.

"Mickey's doesn't open till 10, dumb shit."

"Just fuckin' meet me there. 30 minutes."

Click.

I wouldn't put it past a guy like Henry to set me up or use me to get himself out of a bad way. I sped down the highway and arrived 15 minutes early. I checked under cars for weapons, scoped the parking lot. Mickey's was closed.

I leaned against the building and a limo pulled up.

"Get in." Henry opened the door.

Inside was Henry in his usual cheap lawyer suit, opposite us, a man with a watch worth more than our cars, in a full suit and shoes that looked like mirrors.

"Mr. McIntyre," Henry said, "this is Rick Malone. Your daughter will be in good hands."

Mr. McIntyre sized me up in silence, sipping a coffee, his eyes cold like a man in a high stakes business deal.

"Show him your mitts," Henry said.

I flashed my meat hammers.

Mr. McIntyre turned to Henry. "You don't come highly recommended."

140

"Sir, I know I've had my issues. My associate here will ensure—"

"You vetted the doctor?"

"He's good."

"That's not what I asked."

Henry threw up his hands. "He's got over ten years doing this."

"Again, that's not what I asked."

"Sir," I said, "for what it's worth, I'll do what I can to ensure nothing goes wrong."

He pointed at me. "Wait, you're Mr. Malone, right?"

"He is, Mr.—"

"Was I talkin' to you, Henry?"

"Yes sir," I said.

"There are no guarantees in life," Mr. McIntyre said, "I get that. I also heard how you handled the Kleopatria situation."

"He handles himself—" Henry started.

"Listen, Henry, I don't like you. Every cop, every judge, and almost every politician gets an envelope from me." He leaned in. "Be silent, or I'll make you silent. Are we clear?"

Henry nodded.

"I don't know if I can trust Henry. I think I can trust you."

"Ok."

He threw Henry an envelope and handed me one. "If anything goes wrong, I trust you'll handle it?" He paused. "Go on, Rick. Count it."

I flipped through the bills. $500.

"That's one of my judge's monthly salaries." He handed me and Henry a note with a time, date, and address. "We're done here, Rick."

"Yes sir." I exited the car.

***

Esmerelda said Mr. McIntyre pulled around $150K a month, with $20K going to grease every wheel he could.

"What does he do?" I asked.

"No idea," she said, "but he's always a gentleman when he comes around here. And when he slaps a $50 in my hand? Well, I don't ask questions."

"Safe to assume he's dangerous?"

"How many motherfuckers do you know blow a year's salary each month to keep people in line?"

"Nobody."

"There you go," Esmerelda said. "I don't know what your connection is with him, but Rick, be careful."

I finished my drink and left.

***

Mr. McIntyre lived in a mansion deep in the woods. Following red dirt roads and winding paths, the forest opened up to a sprawling landscape with a fountain and several gardeners tending the bushes and landscape.

I wound around the fountain and killed the engine, got out and buzzed the door.

"Yes?" a voice said.

"Tell Mr. McIntyre Rick Malone is here," I said.

"One second."

A few minutes passed.

"Sir," the voice said, "return to your car. Mary will be out shortly."

I watched the gardeners work, observing their attention to detail, and then I gazed at the mansion. It was as if someone took an apartment complex and structured it into a house. I bet his master bathroom was larger than my apartment.

Mary slumped in the back. "Pleasure to meet you."

"Hello." I started the engine.

"I ain't much for small talk," she said, "can we listen to the radio?"

I flipped on a station playing a song called Sometimes from The Beatles latest album, Abbey Road.

"I love these guys," she said. "I bet they'll put out a dozen more records."

I shifted into drive. "I wouldn't know."

***

After an hour's drive, I parked outside a warehouse in the industrial area. I'd come to learn these procedures don't take long, usually less than half an hour. It had been close to an hour.

I walked over to a payphone a block down, keeping my eye on the car, and dialed Henry.

"What?" he said.

"I'm at a warehouse."

"And this means what?"

"It means you didn't—."

"Quiet," he said, "I don't trust this phone right now."

"I don't give a fuck. Listen—"

Click.

I dialed back.

"What?"

"Henry, you dumbfuck. Don't hang up."

Click.

An hour passed and I rapped on the door.

A white coat with bloodshot eyes answered. "We're not done."

I shoved a gun in his face.

"Hey, hey, hey, listen man. This shit takes time."

"It doesn't. Never takes over 30 mins."

"My nurse is stabilizing her."

"Stabilizing?"

I shoved myself in. "Show me."

He led me through a filthy corridor, the walls bleeding mold. I kicked a rat away.

"If she's in a bad way," I said, "I'll kill you and your nurse. And it won't be quick."

We entered what passed for a medical facility. The nurse was slamming shots of tequila. Blood soaked the table and was dripping on the floor. I checked her pulse and she was barely alive. Passed out.

I shot the nurse and cracked the doctor with the butt of the gun.

"You dumb motherfucker!" I yelled. "You just dug my fuckin' grave." I shot him in the knee. "You even a real fuckin' doctor?"

He clutched his leg and howled. "Few medical classes."

I put two bullets in his skull and grabbed Mary.

Placing her in the back, I jumped in and hit the gas, squealing tires.

***

After actual doctors rushed Mary to a real operating room, I retreated outside and lit a cigarette. I'd promised to keep Mary safe, and when I finished my smoke, I'd call Howard. No doubt I wouldn't live to see morning.

Maybe I should run? Just get in the car, fill it with gas, and head the fuck to Cali. Would anyone really miss me? Would they really put out an APB on my behalf? I smoked hard, staring at my car, and every muscle told me to get in and just drive.

I slumped down, letting smoke curl around my head, trying to figure out all the events that lead to this point, running through a list of what-ifs. I looked at my car once more and hobbled to a payphone.

"Mr. McIntyre." he answered.

"Bad news," I said.

"Rick?"

"It's about Mary."

A long pause made my heart race. I could hear rage-filled breath on the other end.

"Is she dead?"

"She's at St. Vincent's."

"Stay there," he said.

Click.

An hour later, a white Toyota GT 2000GT sped into the lot, and what I assumed was Mrs. McIntyre ran into the hospital. Howard walked behind her in golf clothes and knelt down next to me.

"Where's Henry?"

Sweat poured from my face. "He doesn't know yet."

"Good," he said. "Keep it that way. You did the right thing, calling me."

"I'm sorry."

"The physician?"

"Medical school dropout." I lit another cigarette, assuming it was my last. "He's dead, as is his nurse."

Mr. McIntyre nodded.

"I understand if you want me dead. I won't put up—"

Howard put up a finger then pointed to my car. "You could have run."

I nodded.

"Why didn't you?"

"I don't know."

"It's because you're not a coward," he said. "A lesser man would've ditched. That means something to me."

"I'm very sorry, sir."

"Don't be. This is on Henry." He reached into his pocket and handed me a thick money clip. "If anyone else asks what happened to Mary what do you say?"

"Who's Mary?" I said, "Who's Mr. McIntyre?"

He smiled. "Good. Come by my yacht sometime."

Chapter 25

Towards the end of 1970, Esmerelda called me, ringing me in the middle of the night, rescuing me from nightmares of blood and death.

"Rick," she said, "I need to see you."

"I'll be there in the morning."

"It's urgent."

I sighed. "Fine."

I drove through snow, and a half-drunken stupor to her brothel. My joints ached, and each day more white hairs began appearing. I wasn't getting older, I was old. All these hours on the road, alone in my mind, and all I could think of was Maria and California.

I wish I knew why I didn't just leave, but after a few years, you become robotic. I imagine this is how mafia guys felt being led into a room by their best friend. Why didn't they run? Loyalty? Didn't They know how it would end? Or maybe everything eventually becomes automatic?

So I drive. And throw beat downs. And sometimes I kill. It is what it is I suppose.

I descended the stairs and rapped on the door. Esmerelda answered, her eyes bloodshot. She led me in silence to a back room labeled private. A heart shaped bed, a velvet sofa, and a private bar with lines of cocaine.

Esmerelda stumbled over to the bar, snorted three rails, and slammed a shot of tequila. She slumped down on the couch.

"Why am I here?" I asked.

"You're a good man, Rick." She lit a cigarette and let it dangle from her fingers. "I know what you do, and I don't trust Henry."

"Makes two of us. Why am I here?"

"I have a problem, I need you to handle it."

My face cracked. "I'm tired."

"I am too. It's late. I haven't—"

"Not what I mean. I'm worn out. Since I got out of prison in 66, all I seem to do is threaten people, beat people and fuckin' kill people." I took the liberty of pouring myself a whiskey and slamming it. "I just want something normal."

"Rick," she said, "I get it."

"I don't think you do. I just wanna get the fuck outta here. Just do my time with Henry, go to California, and be a legitimate citizen for once."

She hung her head. "You've always done right by me and my girls. New clients hear your name, and they don't fuck around. Your name carries weight."

"Listen, goddamn it. I'm out. I'll drive for you, but I'm done beatin' people. I'm done killin' people."

Esmerelda took a long drag and started weeping.

"I…I just…I need one last favor, ok?"

"Why should I?"

Desperation bled from her eyes. "I really need you."

I slammed another drink. "Fine, what is it?"

"It's a big one."

Driver

My face soured and I lit a cigarette. "Lay it on me."

***

I drove down the icy road in silence. A John got one of Esmerelda's girls pregnant, and since she didn't trust Henry, took it upon herself to find someone. This someone turned out to be another medical school dropout. Esmerelda knew this, and maybe it was the booze or blow, but she trusted this person.

Minnie Quinn. Late 20s. Hairdresser by day, illegal abortion provider by night. Esmerelda gave me her address, and she knew her work schedule. I checked my watch. 2AM. She'd leave her house at 8AM. Christ. Six hours to wait.

I parked a few houses down and killed the engine. My eyes betrayed me, and I fell asleep.

I jolted awake with a hangover. 8:30AM. Her car was gone. "Goddamn it."

"I just wanna go to California!" I screamed, banging my hands on the steering wheel. "Fuck this shit."

Minnie worked 8:30-4:30. Henry had nothing planned for that day, so I drove over to the cemetery and collapsed by Maria's grave. No letter this time.

"I hope you don't see what I've become."

My eyes fell heavy again, and everything went black.

I felt the poke of a stick.

"What?" I said, looking up at an old man in groundskeeper clothes.

"Get up."

"What time is it?"

"Almost five. Why?"

"Thanks," I said, "Sorry for falling asleep."

"Sir, you're reeking of booze." He looked offended. "This is a cemetery. Have you no respect?"

"Again, I'm sorry."

***

I lit a cigarette and waited outside Minnie's house. Esmerelda said she was single and I didn't see another car in the driveway. I checked my watch. Close to Six.

She wanted me to report back by noon. She probably thought I skipped town. I refused to call her. When this was done, I was done. No more driving for her. Just serve out my time with Henry, and leave.

I got out and approached her house and knocked.

"Can I help you?" she said with the door half cracked.

"Ma'am," I said, "I'm a private detective. I'm following up on a lead. May I come in?"

"Sure."

People are too trusting. We sat at the table, and she brought me a cup of coffee.

"What's this about?" she asked.

I sighed, removing my gun and setting it on the table. "Don't scream."

Her face turned white.

"I don't have money, sir." She started crying. "I have an infant son."

I hung my head. "You know Esmerelda, right?"

"Oh god."

"Just a yes or no."

She nodded.

I pointed my stone face at her. "I'm sure we know how this is gonna end."

She nodded again.

"How do you want to die?"

"What?"

"How do you want to die?" I asked.

"Can I write my son a letter first?"

I nodded.

I smoked two cigarettes while her shaky hands penned the letter. She folded it up and placed it on the side of the table. She never begged. Never tried to reason with me. It's almost as if she knew her fate was sealed. Or maybe my reputation permeated her skin.

"Tell Esmerelda she's a real bitch."

I nodded.

"I only ever tried to do right," she said, "My son is sleeping. I don't want him to find me. Bring me to the basement?"

I nodded, and she led the way down the stairs.

I positioned myself behind her, my knife against her throat. "Alright Mama, I'm comin' home."

***

I waited until she stopped twitching and stepped over the pool of blood. Upon reaching the top, I heard a woman's voice.

"Minnie, just coming down for a snack."

I recognized the voice. Sounded like one of Esmerelda's girls.

I entered the kitchen and the girl jumped.

"Rick," she said, "what are you doing here?"

"I could ask the same." I leaned against the counter. "You pregnant?"

"No, why?"

"Why are you here?"

"Please," she said, "don't tell Esmerelda."

"Tell her what?"

"I don't fancy being a prostitute no more. I told her, but she'd have nothing of it. I brought in too much money."

"Hang on," I said, "Is Minnie a medical school dropout?"

"I don't think so," she said, "But she was helping me get away from Esmerelda." She paused. "Where's Minnie?"

"Listen carefully," I said, "ok?"

She nodded.

"Do you have the resources to leave?"

"Sure," she said, "Minnie had it all set up. We were going to the airport tomorrow."

"Do not go in the basement."

"Why?"

"Just don't."

"Is Minnie down there?"

"Listen," I said, "You never saw me. Pack what you have, and we'll go to the airport tonight."

"Why?"

"I need you to do what I tell you. Please. It's for your own good."

She nodded.

"Pack what you need. I'll give you five minutes."

She nodded again and went upstairs. I grabbed the letter, read it, and shoved it in my pocket.

I dialed Esmerelda.

"It's done," I said when she answered.

"Took you long enough. Jesus fuckin' Christ."

"I'll swing by in about an hour, ok?"

"Sure."

The girl came down with a suitcase, and we headed down the road. I saw a payphone close to the airport, and called in the murder, indicating there was a sleeping boy in the house.

"Remember," I said pulling up at the gates, "you never saw me. Forget about me. Forget about Esmerelda. Ok?"

She nodded.

"Get goin' now."

I watched her vanish into the airport.

I hit the gas when I saw her plane penetrate the sky.

***

My blood boiled driving back to Esmerelda's. I wanted to burn through every stop light, kick in the door, and shoot her in the head.

I descended the stairs and saw two new guys at Esmerelda's place. Both looked unarmed.

"Appointment?" one asked.

"The fuck outta my way," I said. "I work for Esmerelda."

"Sir—" one started

I jammed my gun in his mouth. "I'm in no fuckin' mood. Get the fuck out my fuckin' way."

I opened the door and locked it behind me.

"Mr. Malone," the bartender said. "Good to see you. Can I—"

"Where's Esmerelda?"

"I'm here," she said. "Follow me."

We returned to the room with the private bar. The cocaine was gone, and Esmerelda looked like she hadn't slept in days.

"It's done?"

"It's done. And I'm out."

"I know, no more killings."

"No, I'm out. I don't ever wanna hear from you ever again, we clear?"

She shook her head. "You saw, didn't you?"

"I'm out. Lose my number."

"Rick, I'm sorry I tricked you. I really—"

I clenched my fist. "Shut your mouth, or I'll shut it for you."

"Darling," she said, "I got dirt on Henry. Stay, maybe I can make it up to you."

I grabbed a bottle of Macallan 1926 whiskey from the bar.

"Put that down," she said. "That's aged 60 years. I charge $700 a glass."

I poured myself a glass and smashed the bottle on the bar.

"You dumb motherfucker," she said.

I slammed the drink. "Tastes like shit anyway."

"You just burned a powerful ally."

"Nah." I pointed the gun at Esmerelda. "I don't think so. What do you have on Henry?"

"Like I'm gonna tell you now. What? Gonna shoot me? Go for it..."

"Then I guess you get a closed casket."

"In the old west," she said, "people like me ran towns. Nobody fucked with a brothel owner."

"This ain't the old west, bitch."

"You kill me, you won't make it five fuckin' blocks before the cops charged you with every last motherfuckin' thing they can think of." She smirked, rage flaring in her eyes, as if Napoleon himself had fallen from grace. "Well, assuming you make downtown. Which. I. Doubt."

"Maybe so," I said. "But before they pick me up, this place is going up in smoke, with you in it."

"You *save the world* people," she said, a sneering contempt in her voice.

"Give me the dirt on Henry." I paused, lighting a cigarette. "And I leave all peaceful like." I paused. "Oh, and I got a letter from Minnie. It's to her son, but she names you, and names how you hired someone to kill her."

"You son of a bitch."

"Yeah, well, I've been called worse. Spill the fuckin' beans, and if anything happens to me? Well, you'll go down too."

Chapter 26

We were close to entering the city and my last ride was coming to a close. Each ride I'd imagine what my life could have been. If Maria hadn't died, would I have been a successful race car driver? Would we be in California, right now, relaxing on the beach? Perhaps in an alternate universe, we were. Maybe right now, an alternate me, and an alternate Maria were sipping drinks, watching the waves come in and out. And sometimes, a racing fan would ask for my autograph. Hell, maybe they'd even hit me up to do chase scenes like Steve McQueen did in Bullitt.

"Piece of advice?" I asked.

"Sure."

"When this is all over." I paused, holding back tears. "Stay off drugs. Even booze."

"Ok?"

"Sorry," I said, "I guess… just promise you won't end up like me."

"But you're a good man, Rick." Elizabeth touched my arm. "I can see it."

"No. I'm not. I'm a fuck up."

"Oh Rick," she said, "nobody's perfect, least of all me."

I rolled up my sleeve and displayed the scars from burnt out veins. "Don't be like me."

"Heroin?"

I nodded. "From my teens until—" A tear rolled down my cheek. "Until Maria."

158

"I'm sorry, Rick."

"Don't be. It is what it is."

"What did it feel like?"

"Heroin?"

She nodded.

I lit a cigarette and took a drag. "The first time felt like a mother's warm hug."

Chapter 27

I was 23 when Maria stumbled over my half dead carcass. At this point, I was shooting up every two hours to feel human. Veins in both arms had collapsed, as did the ones in my right leg. My left had maybe two good veins left.

"Buddy," Maria said, "You don't look so hot."

Looking up, a poem of a woman stood before me. Long auburn locks, a flowing blue dress with white high heels. Light radiated from her eyes.

"You'll freeze to death out here," she said.

That was the plan. I'd been searching for oblivion for years, contorting myself day after day to forget who I was. Just a few hours where I didn't have to be me.

"You can't stay out here," she said, "let's get you to a hospital."

"I'm fine," I said, vomit caking my beard.

"I insist."

***

I woke up in the hospital and Maria said I'd been out for a few days. They flushed my system and apparently during the detox they kickstarted my heart.

I felt like shit and no doubt smelled even worse. When I looked over, I saw Maria in a checkered circle shirt tucked into blue jeans. She was reading a book. I'd find out later the book was Richard Wright's Native Son. Reading it decades later, I wondered, how much of my life is like Bigger Thomas?

"You're awake," Maria said. "I was worried."

"Why?"

She closed her book. "Why what?"

"Why were you worried?"

"I mean, you almost died out there. And in here."

"But why did you care?"

"Because too many people don't."

"You stuck around," I said. "Why?"

She shrugged, then smiled. "Many people don't."

"You're not—" I paused, feeling nauseous. "You're not some, I dunno, save-the-world Christian are you?"

She laughed. "No."

"I don't get why you're here. Why you care."

"It's ok," she said. "Maybe it's because I know what it's like when people don't care."

I threw up in the trash can.

"Sorry," I said.

"Darling," she chuckled. "I've seen a lot worse."

"You seem like a nice girl. You do. Maybe you shouldn't waste time on me."

She leaned in and her face lit up. "It's my time to waste."

***

When they released me from the hospital, Maria gave me her phone number and said to call.

"Call you for what?" I shrunk into the outside bench, unsure of why she was hanging around.

"If you need to talk." She sat down beside me. "You got a place to stay?"

"I'll be ok."

I could see her looking down at my heroin scorched arms. I expected a lecture. I expected her to bombard me with platitudes on how bad drugs are. But she didn't do that. Maybe she knew I wouldn't be receptive. Or maybe she knew something deeper: soft words and kind gestures are better substitutes.

She got up to leave. "You be good now, ok?"

I nodded.

Weeks passed, and I never called her. I'd wander past payphones and hold back picking up the ringer. My detox quickly devolved into old habits of shooting heroin, vomiting in trash cans and burning out more veins.

"You'll never make it to 25," a homeless woman told me.

"Why's that?" I asked.

"I see how much you take." She hawked up mucus. "They say 200mg is a lethal dose. Pal, I see you take that every few hours." She looked down at my legs. "You got what, one good vein left?"

I stumbled over to Chicago's DuSable Bridge, with a needle filled with three times my usual dose. My plan was to inject, jump, and drift off into permanent oblivion.

Cars passed on a sunny afternoon, paying no attention to a bum. I looked over the side into the water. I remember my dad's wrench to my back. I remember not remembering where they were buried. Gazing into the water below, I savored my last moments. For the first time I realized I didn't have to hold on so tight. I was 23, and peace washed over me as I removed the syringe.

"Rick," a voice called out. Maria? I turned around and saw her approaching.

"Yeah, Rick, admiring the view, eh?"

I nodded.

"Mind if I join you?"

"I'd rather you didn't."

She leaned against a rail beside me. "Too bad, cowboy. I want to admire the view too."

I hung my head. "Please leave."

She took out a full pack of cigarettes, cracked it open and lit up. "I have all day."

"You're going to smoke 20 cigarettes here?"

She chuckled. "I'd rather not. But if I have to, I will."

"It's best if you leave."

"You want one?"

"Ok," I said, taking a cigarette she lit and inhaling deeply. "After this, please leave."

She slapped the rail. "Hey, want to hear a joke?"

I stared into the river refusing to gaze upon her. "I guess."

She started laughing before starting. "Oh man, you'll love this one. What do you call a door-to-door bra salesman?" She paused, waiting for me to guess. I didn't. "The fuller bust man."

She burst out laughing, slapping the rail, and some people looked on. I think they overheard.

I cracked a grin. "Not bad."

We stood in silence for a bit and my cigarette was almost done. I took a final drag and flung it into the river.

"Ok," I said, "I need you to leave now."

She lit another. "Nah, think I'll stay."

"Listen." My hands shook. "I don't want to be mean. You're a nice girl. But—"

"Well thank you." She grinned. "I have my moments."

"—But get the fuck outta here."

She flung off her shoes and looked into the river.

"Guess we do this together, eh?"

"You're gonna jump?"

"Sure, why not? You're going to."

"Lady." I slapped the railing. "Just fuckin' leave, ok? Please."

She inhaled and put her hand on my back. "No."

***

She stood next to me and smoked half a pack of cigarettes before I realized she wasn't going to leave. We left the bridge and got in her rusty bucket car. My hands started shaking. It'd been a few hours since my last hit.

"Go ahead," she said, leaning against the car. "Shoot up. We'll get you clean at my place."

I plunged half the dose and stumbled into the passenger seat.

She entered the driver's seat. "One more joke, ok?"

I nodded.

"A man went to a doctor. Said he was depressed, real down and out. Couldn't sleep. Felt lonely and miserable."

"I know about that."

"The doctor said: I know what'll cheer you up. The famous comedian Johnny Walker is in town. He makes everybody laugh. That's just what you need. The man burst into tears: but I am Johnny Walker."

Maria laughed, and everything went black.

***

The first week at Maria's place was a blur. Lots of vomiting, insomnia, and felt like the flu hit me like a train.

I stumbled to a mirror, looking at my trainwreck of a body. Sunken face, skin hanging off bone, my face drained of blood. I cleaned up in the shower and slumped into bed.

Maria pulled up a chair. "Rough few days, eh?"

"What do you do?"

"Besides getting you clean?" she said, cradling a cup of coffee.

I nodded.

"I shelve books at the Newberry Library."

"A librarian."

She shook her head. "I wish. I stock books. It pays the bills."

"Sounds lovely."

"What are your dreams?"

"Cars." I suppressed the urge to vomit. "Maybe be a race car driver. Maybe race in films someday."

"I know a mechanic," she said. "I'll introduce you."

"Why are you nice to me?"

She cocked her head and smiled. "Maybe I see something in you that you don't see."

***

Weeks rolled into months and months rolled into a small chapel wedding. Maria didn't say much about her family, nor did I talk about mine. Atop a hill, amidst empty pews, except for the mechanic I worked for Mickey O'Toole, a priest married us.

After, Mickey went back to work, and we wandered the forest.

"Someday," I smiled, "I'll give you a proper honeymoon."

"I want to see California," she said, kissing me while birds chirped in the trees.

"Why California?" I cracked a smile.

"It's the state they call the City of Angels, right?"

"Los Angeles?"

"Since I was a girl I wanted to see it." She closed her eyes and breathed in deep. "I want to feel the sand on my feet and the waves crash against me."

I pulled her closer for another kiss.

"Promise we'll go someday?"

I nodded. "Of course."

***

About a year into working for Mickey, he approached while I was bent over a 41 Chevrolet Coupe working on the fuel line.

"Rick," he said, wiping grease from his hands. "You've been doin' real good here."

Oh shit. I'm doing real good, but I'm about to be fired, aren't I?

"Listen here," he said, "your wife has been calling me every week."

I chuckled. "What?"

"Yeah, bustin' my balls about juicing you in as a racecar driver."

"Every week?" I asked.

"Goddamn," he laughed. "For months."

I leaned against the car and lit a cigarette. "She's persistent. Believe me. I know."

He pointed to a red Porsche 356. "You like that?"

I took a drag. "Been eyeing it for weeks."

"Good," he said and slapped me on the back. "It's yours."

My eyes grew wide. "No shit?"

"Not free and clear. I'll take payments out of your salary." He paused. "A week from now, about an hour north of here, there's an open race."

"Legal?"

Mickey sighed. "As legal as it can get. I have no doubt some mob bookie peckerwoods will be there."

"What's the prize?"

"First place gets you $200. Second gets you $100. Third nets you $50." He wiped sweat from his forehead. "And of course I'll plaster the Mickey's Garage logo on the driver and passenger doors." He winked. "You know, good advertisement."

I extended my hand. "Thank you."

His greasy palms melded with mine. "Thank Maria. You got a helluva good woman there, Rick."

***

Even practicing for a week, I still came in last with no prize money. The other guys were seasoned racers, and all the girls crowded around them. Maria hung on my arm.

"Ya win some," she said, resting her head on my shoulder. "Ya lose some. Cheer up, darling."

As much as I wanted to wallow in self-pity, the streets taught me many people never get even one good thing. The lot of them was misery from cradle to an early grave. But I have Maria, and that's as good as it gets.

My face turned sour. "They look happy."

"Don't be such a sour puss." She slugged me in the arm and pointed to the second-place winner. "That's Frank Jackson. He's been doing this for almost a decade."

Chicago turned my stomach. I didn't want to ever return. California sounded better and better each day.

"You know," I said, "wanna skip town? Just take this fuckin' car and go to California?"

"Fuckin' car?" she laughed. "The car fucks?"

I wiped sweat from my brow. "You know what I mean."

"We will," she smiled. "But not today."

"Why?"

She cupped my face. "Rick, my love, you can't run from life. California won't fix the battle behind your eyes."

I kissed her and rested my head on her shoulders. "Before we turn thirty, ok?"

"Ok."

"Promise?"

"I promise."

Chapter 28

Elizabeth started fidgeting with a rosary. "Think I should do it?"

"Not for me to say."

"You're family," she said, "I don't know what to do."

What would Maria want me to say? Moments like this convinced me the wrong person got cancer, and the wrong person died. Maria would know how to answer without judgment or condemnation. Elizabeth used the word family as if we both didn't know that meant nothing.

"Rick?"

"Sorry," I said, "I just…"

"What would you do?"

Get the fuck out of Illinois, and go somewhere warm, where the waves could wash away the memories.

"I'm trying to think what Maria would say."

"If I return, still pregnant…" she trailed off.

"I know."

"But I don't know. Maybe I would be a good mother? What do you think?"

"Elizabeth," my voice cracked. "Maria and I never talked of having children. But I think if we did, we'd want someone like you."

She rubbed the rosary harder. "If I keep the baby, can I stay with you?"

A tear rolled down my cheek. "No."

"Oh, I understand."

Another tear. "No, it's not that. It's just…"

"Just what?"

"I've done certain things. Bad things. Things a man doesn't recover from."

"Such as?"

"You're well read, right?"

She nodded.

"I've crossed the Rubicon." I paused and looked at the clock. Fifteen minutes until our arrival. "I just…"

"For what it's worth, I think you'd have made a great dad." She smiled. "You're sure you can't be a grandpa?"

"I'm sorry," I said, holding tears back.

Chapter 29

In the summer and fall of 72, Henry's contacts killed several women, and left more women reproductively fucked. People would call in the middle of the night. Politicians. Oil men. Anyone on the right side of capitalism, to threaten me.

"Make this right, or I'll put out a bounty on your fuckin' mick head!" one guy said. I could almost feel the spit through the phone.

I answered and one guy started yelling before I could say hello. "You fuck. You'll fuckin' pay for this in blood. You fucked with the wrong family."

These calls continued until I called each back and said: We need to meet to work this out.

When I stepped aboard Mr. McIntyre's yacht, my stomach screamed: you'll never see Chicago again. A part of me hoped this was the end.

Mr. McIntyre handed me a drink and told me to sit. Five men showed up, and we sailed off into lake Michigan.

"Gentlemen," Mr. McIntyre said, "Rick did my family right a while back. My daughter is alive because of him."

A man's face turned red. "Good for you. Mine's dead because of this prick."

Mr. McIntyre walked over and smacked him across the face. "You forget who the fuck you're talkin' to, senator." He leaned in. "I can make you disappear. Show some goddamn respect."

The man lit a cigar. "So now what?"

"Yeah!" the others chimed in.

"We clean house," Mr. McIntyre said. "Rick's the man for the job. And you five make sure he does. Call in whatever favors needed."

"Fuck favors," another guy said. "Rick owes us."

"No," Mr. McIntyre said, "he doesn't." He looked at me. "You'll make it right?"

"Yes sir," I said.

Mr. McIntyre smiled. "Good. You boys want your vengeance or not?"

***

When we docked, the men got off, but Mr. McIntyre told me to stay. He poured us both a drink, and I lit a cigarette.

"When this is done," he said, "I want you to find someone legitimate."

I inhaled and downed the liquid. Even for my throat it burned. "May I be blunt?"

He nodded.

"I just want to serve my time with Henry, then get the fuck outta here."

He eyed the liquid in his glass. "That wasn't a request. But you'll be compensated nicely."

"Compensate me by dealing with Henry."

He grunted. "If I do that, I'll end up in the wall of a skyscraper."

I took a drag, defeat washing over me. "I just want to go to California."

"I like you, Rick. I really do." He downed his drink. "When you get to Cali, gimme a ring. I do business there." He paused. "Just leave Henry alone. He's a fuck up, I know. But he's the bosses fuck up. Serve your time. How much longer?"

"Few more years," I said. "I'll be over 50."

He handed me a folder. "A dossier. You have three days, and carte blanche to do whatever to these people." He leaned in, his eyes liquid nitrogen. "And only these people. We clear?"

"Crystal."

Chapter 30

Returning to my apartment, I brewed a pot of coffee and cracked open the dossier. Three groups, located in various shitholes around Chicago. One could argue Chicago is one big festering shithole.

Thomas "Lysol" Richards. 42. Revoked medical license (though they don't say why). His MO was pumping plant poison and Lysol up the vaginal cavity.

A husband-and-wife team: Richard and Martha Johnson, 27, and 25. Richard finished medical school at the bottom of his class, but never finished his clinicals. Martha is a Registered Nurse, and in good standing with the medical community. The reports indicate she has an impeccable record.

The last guy, a real jerk-off, Samuel Miller, 21. No medical training except it's claimed he studied textbooks. No college or higher educational experience, but a lengthy criminal record. Petty theft, vandalism, and aggravated assault which lead to his incarceration from 13-18.

I closed the file, committing the addresses to memory. I smoked a few cigarettes and drank the pot of coffee before visiting Maria's grave.

Stumbling through the cemetery, I brought a different shape of grief.

Another note by her headstone.

Dear Maria,

I'm in a bad way. I'm pregnant, and I don't know what to do. I don't really have the motherly instinct. But something inside me (besides the life that grows), bonds me somehow.

Mom and Dad arranged something, but they didn't tell me much. I'm scared and alone. I never asked God for anything, but maybe you can tell him to send an angel. I don't know what I did to deserve all this. I really wish I could have met you.

Best,

Nobody.

My next client?

"Sorry Maria," I said, "I can't stay."

I dialed a nearby payphone.

"What?" Henry rasped.

"When's my next thing?"

"Next week."

"Thanks."

"Why do—"

Click.

Three days max to eliminate Henry's contacts, and six to find a reputable physician.

***

Thomas left his Suburban house as the sun came up. He chatted up his neighbors, before heading down the road. As best I can tell, Thomas did this full-time. He had an air of respectability, wearing a gray suit and gold tie. Men in suits bamboozle the American imagination. If a man wears a suit, he *must* be respectable, right?

We drove through industrial districts, until we arrived outside Chicago at a secluded cabin. Parked in an inconspicuous spot and watched a nurse park outside the cabin.

Before I could storm the place, two men exited the cabin, buff, like titty bar bouncers.

I made my way to the street, assuming a client would show up. A rusted-out car started turning down the road, and I waved them down. An older man, younger woman.

"You Dr. Richards?" the man asked.

"His assistant," I said. "Didn't he call you?"

"No?" the man said, his face scrunched. "Why?"

I leaned in. "Dr. Richards is under the weather. Some kind of stomach bug I think."

"Ah shit," the man said. "Should I call and reschedule?"

"No need. He'll call you in a few days. He apologizes for the inconvenience and told me to tell anyone who shows up he'll offer a discount for your troubles."

The man nodded. "Sure, we can wait a few days. Dr. Richards comes highly recommended. Hope he feels better."

The man backed up and disappeared into the horizon.

Returning to my car, I had maybe 30 minutes until someone else showed up. I grabbed my knife and checked my pistol. Six rounds.

As I approached the cabin, the two bouncers approached.

"Hey," one said, "you're not—"

I shot him and his buddy in the head.

"The fuck's goin' on out there?" a voice echoed from the cabin.

The nurse ran out, and I shot her in the chest, then the head.

Thomas emerged in scrubs. "Jesus Christ."

I finished my clip into him.

I ran back to my car and peeled off down the road.

***

On my way to the Johnson's, red and blue lights appeared in my rearview. Pulling over, palms became wet, and whatever residual heroin in my system was sweated out as the officer approached.

The cop knocked on the window.

"What can I do for you, Officer?"

"The Johnsons are skipping town." He handed me a new address. "I assume you know who I work for. Go here instead."

"Skipping town?"

"You got two hours before the Feds show up." He tapped his watch. "Work quickly, then get out."

Goddamn it. The address was, in ideal traffic, at least an hour away.

I stepped on the gas and took side streets. Rolled up and checked my watch. Ten minutes. I grabbed my gun, but before I could make a move, the Feds descended on the house.

I slammed my fist on the dash. "Fuck. Fuck. Fuck!!"

***

Catching Miller alone took me until the third day. He'd hit up pimps, hang out in crowded bars, he almost got arrested for assault when I pulled up and told him to get in.

I hit the gas.

"Thanks man," he said. "Dunno who you are, but thanks. I owe you one, pal."

When the cops saw my car, they pulled away, but I kept on the gas until we were outside the city limits.

"Fuck man," he said, "we lost em. We're good now."

Shooting him in the car would blow out my ear drums, and obviously make too much of a mess.

"Step outside and enjoy a smoke?" I asked.

He shrugged. "Sure man."

We lit up and leaned against the car. The sun set in the distance, and amid all the violence, and filth in the city, I glimpsed beauty painting the sky.

"Not often you enjoy a sunset, eh?"

I took a drag.

"Life's short," he continued. "Gotta take time to smell—"

I pushed him away from the car and double tapped him in the back of the head.

Returning home, I drank a bottle of whiskey, almost passed out in the shower and crashed on my bed. I picked up a picture of Maria posing by a winter light pole.

"I'm glad you're not around to see who I am."

***

The next day, we all convened on Mr. McIntyre's yacht.

"Problem solved," Mr. McIntyre said. "Compensate Rick."

The five men huddled. The one in a fancy suit, the senator, spoke for the group. "He didn't kill the Johnsons."

"The Feds nabbed 'em," I said. "They're not a problem anymore."

"That's right." Mr. McIntyre lit a cigar. "We sent a message."

"I don't want them in prison," the senator said. "I want them fucking dead!"

"Can't always get what you want," I said.

The senator turned to Mr. McIntyre. "Why is this piece of white trash even here?"

My face turned cold. "You fellas carry guns?"

They shook their heads.

I took out my pistol and pointed it at the senator.

"Good."

"Woah, Rick," Mr. McIntyre said. "Relax."

I walked over to the senator and grabbed him by the tie.

"Piece,"

Crack to the nose,

"Of,"

Crack to the nose,

"White,"

Crack to the nose,

"Trash."

I sat back down, my arms shaking, blood soaking the senator's suit, admiring the blood spraying from his face, and his nose crooked. "Any more of you caviar suckin' maggots got somethin' smart to say?"

"You fucked up, son," one of the men said.

"You're fuckin' dead," the senator managed to say. "You won't make it past the day. You're dead! You're fuckin' dead!"

Mr. McIntyre snapped his fingers. "Fork over the envelopes." He winked at me. "Don't make Rick rearrange anymore faces."

***

The men departed the boat and Mr. McIntyre handed me two of the three envelopes.

"Sorry," I said.

"I'll smooth things over," he said, "but you gotta get out of town, and never return."

"I need a week."

"Why a week?"

"One last job."

"Gimme back an envelope."

"Why?"

He snapped his fingers. "It'll buy you a week."

Chapter 31

"You had to have known," Elizabeth said.

"Pardon?"

"That you and I are related."

I lit the second to last cigarette. "Why's that?"

"I left dozens of letters at Maria's grave." She started tearing up. "You must have stumbled upon some."

I nodded. "I told you I did."

"I'm scared, Rick." She rubbed her crucifix. "I don't know what to do, I just know I want you to be there whatever I choose."

"I will."

"No, I mean, beyond today."

"You know what would make me happy?" I asked.

"What?"

"Whatever happens, don't let one man kill your dreams." I took a drag. "Become a mathematician."

She hung her head. "It's funny, my father gained wealth, but I'll always be white trash."

I snapped my fingers. "No. No. Don't ever say that."

"The sad truth, Rick? They'll never accept me. Not really. Girls don't amount to much. Girls don't become mathematicians."

"Elizabeth," I said, "Maria wasn't a violent person. But…she'd slap you upside the head for saying that."

She burst out laughing. "A real firecracker was she?"

"Ohhhh, Elizabeth." I took a long drag, and kept tears locked inside. "I wish you could'a met her."

She smiled. "Well, I got you."

"Yeah…"

Chapter 32

A few days before I picked up Elizabeth, I met Dr. Rita Wilson at her family practice, sandwiched between a church and an adult bookstore. The stop sign before her clinic was riddled with bullet holes. A burnt car rusted down the way.

The night before she slipped a folder under my door with a note:

Mr. Malone,

You need someone reliable.

We should meet.

My number's inside.

Half confession, half resume, the dossier revealed Dr. Wilson didn't use coat hangers or knitting needles. She didn't pump the women full of Lysol or plant poison. And, somehow, despite the odds of being black, graduated top of her class at Johns Hopkins in the late 50s. Despite the procedure being illegal, her dossier included the names of another physician, Don Philips, anesthesiologist, as well as two surgical nurses, Mary Jane and Sarah Jackson. The file listed them as respectable members of the medical community. In all my years working for Henry, not a single abortionist had an anesthesiologist. Only one had a nurse.

Catholic paraphernalia littered her office like children's toys at the county morgue. I walked around, transfixed by the statues of saints, the rosary made of precious gems, and a reprint of a painting of The Immaculate Conception by Bartolomé Esteban Murillo.

"Ironic," I said, nodding at the painting. "Maria was a fan of Murillo."

"Your wife?"

I nodded.

"Surprised I'm Catholic?" Dr. Wilson asked.

I sat down and thumbed through the file.

"Impressive file. You're an actual doctor." My eyes filled with ice. "That don't mean much in my world, though."

"Look, if it needs to be done, it needs to be done right. And with care." She lit a Newport. "I don't like what I do, it goes against everything I believe. But it is what it is, ya know? And what's the alternative? These med school dropouts? Or, worse, the ones with suspended licenses and fat malpractice files? Not sure which class of degenerate is worse."

Sirens blared in consistent intervals. A gunshot rang out. A woman cried for help. This should have startled me. This should have made them run, but before entering the clinic, I stepped over a body, and before that, drove past a stop sign with three bullet holes, and before that, a car bomb illuminated a side street.

She took a long drag. "They market this to us, ya know." She exhaled through her nostrils. "Gotta love the slogan: Alive With Pleasure. 'Suppose it's better marketing than: Dead Niggers Forever." She let out a cackle. "This whole crazy world is—"

"You reliable?" I snapped the file shut.

Her face hung like the slow ticking of a grandfather clock. "Last week a woman came into my practice—a sweet, precious thing, something God made, a fever of 103. She damn near died o' heat stroke. You know what I found? A rubber catheter in her cervix." She took another drag and exhaled. "Let that sink in. And every week I see hatchet jobs like this. These people are like children fumbling with chainsaws." She puffed harder. "And every week I grow more and more goddamn sick of it."

"Why am I only hearing about you now?"

She scrunched her face. "Surely you know Henry ain't no fan of negroes." She paused. "I offered my services. He hung up when he found out how much melanin was in my skin."

"How'd she turn out?" I asked as if I expected something happy.

"Who?"

"The girl."

Dr. Wilson stared at the wall, as though the nicotine stains would divine some answers. As if the Virgin Mary mural would reveal God's unvirgin plan. "Told her she couldn't have children. Too much cervical damage." She closed her eyes. "She slit her wrists the next day."

"Sorry to hear that."

"Yeah," Dr. Wilson said. "All too common. Shall I continue explaining why I do—"

"No."

"Who'da thunk we'd be outlaws?" She cracked a window, a cool breeze flooded in. "Folks like us always return to the streets. Our souls are tethered to it, rusted chains we hate, then learn to love." She paused. "At least I get a 9-5 paycheck."

"Are you reliable?"

"What's yer favorite color?"

"Don't have one."

"Food?"

"Whatever Maria made."

"Who? Oh never mind, your wife," she said, "And did you choose to love her cooking? Or did it choose you?"

"Lady, listen, time's valuable. Are you—"

"You know Rick, let me tell you somethin'. It don't matter that I went to Johns Hopkins. It don't matter that I graduated at the top of my class." She exhaled a cloud of smoke. "People never see the white coat. You know what they see?"

"Someone who talks too much?"

"Hardy-fuckin'har." She extended her arm and rubbed it. "This. That's it."

"Listen lady, I—"

"The point, Mr. Malone, is that the outlaw lifestyle chose us, not the other way around. You don't have to like it. You can downright hate it. I know I do. But it likes *you*. It likes *me*. Ya feel?"

"You contacted me, said you were reliable. Another time, another place, I might entertain philosophical ramblings, but right now, I need someone who will do these girls right." I leaned back. "How'd ya find me anyway?"

"The streets sing your name." She laughed, lighting up another Newport. "The streets say yer a failed race-car driver, they also say you were about to make it big, say your wife was lovely too. Boy oh boy, life sure took a left turn off a cliff." A car backfired, or maybe it was another gunshot. "How many times has your soul broke? Has it shattered yet? Will all the king's horsemen and all the king's men—"

"No." I lit a cigarette.

"Word 'round these parts is Thomas Richards's doin' time in the ICU because o' you." A smile shattered her face. "Ya took care of what I couldn't. For six months I've been tryin' to put that cocksucker outta business."

"He's dead."

A smile cracked her face. "Good. Fuck him."

"I don't suffer incompetence." I took a drag and exhaled through my nostrils. "You understand?"

She nodded. "You won't find anyone better."

"Because if you're not reliable," I said, "you'll end up in a bad way."

"My team knows the golden rule. Keep your mouth shut except at the dentist."

I nodded. "Demand double from Henry."

"I already did." She smirked, the Newport dangling from her lips. "You get what you pay for."

I nodded.

"My time's endin'," Dr. Wilson said. "Rumor has it this will all be on the up and up." She tossed me The New York Times. "Been followin' the Roe v. Wade case?"

"I've heard," I said, "but, right now, are you reliable?"

"Bring her to me. I'll do it right." She paused. "My team will do 'em right."

"Ma'am, for your sake, I hope so."

"Ma'am? I'm movin' up in the world. Streets never said you a gentleman."

"I ain't."

Rita patted her St. Jude statue. "You'll not find a better team."

"For your sake," I patted my revolver. "I hope so."

Chapter 33

The day before I met my last client, I kicked open Henry's door. "They're all dead."

"The whores?" Henry asked, puffing on a Cohibas. "Say what ya will about that pinko commie Castro, he knows his cigars."

"Ya listening, ya fuck? Your contacts." I flung a picture of a mangled vagina at Henry's face. Then another, and another. "The people who did this all fuckin' dead."

Henry puffed harder. "You motherfucker. Crime is built into your DNA, ain't it boy?"

"I pick the provider. We clear?"

"Or, perhaps I call—"

I pointed to the window. "Touch the phone and I'll put your brain to sleep."

Henry grabbed a shotgun. "You fuckin' people don't know yer fuckin' place. I don't know what's worse. You or the goddamn niggers I gotta deal with."

"I know the church you and your wife attend. St. Boniface Cathedral, downtown, 7:30am, every Sunday." I took out an envelope and slid it across the desk. "And I happen to know that every Friday you meet a sexy blonde bombshell. I even talked to her. Washed up Honduran model turned prostitute, no? Mole on her left cheek?"

"Hey, fuck you. Just fuck you and fuck yer dead wife. Who da fuck you think—"

"I happen to know she's also mob connected." I paused. "She don't much like you, say's you're a bit rough. Perhaps I tell her to tell the bosses you slap her around?"

Henry slumped down in his chair. "What's the provider's name?"

"Fuck you, that's her name." I grabbed the shotgun. "Just tell me where and when."

"Are we done?"

"Almost," I said, strapping on a pair of brass knuckles. "You're gonna take the beatin' we both know you deserve."

A pool of urine pooled under Henry.

"In my world," I said, cracking him on the jaw, blood spraying the wall. "Incompetence is paid for in blood."

Chapter 34

With enough cash to get out of Chicago and the clock ticking, I wanted a clean bill of health. Tomorrow I'd pick up my last girl, then hit the road for California. At my age, racing dreams were out of the question, but maybe Hollywood needed a stuntman. Maybe the Pacific could wash away the broken bottles in my brain.

The doctor returned to the room and sat down. "Bad news."

"Ok."

"You haven't been getting headaches, feeling dizzy, short of breath?"

"Yeah," I said, "I chalked it up to being old."

"There's no nice way of saying this," he said, lighting a cigarette. "You have advanced cancer."

"How advanced?"

"You gotta be a tough ol' boy," he said, "I'm really sorry. It's a hell of a thing."

"The kind you don't recover from?"

"No. You have maybe a month at most."

One last ride. One last girl. Then one month of memories before I die on a Pacific beach.

***

I returned home to my phone ringing.

"Hello?"

"Get your ass down here," Henry said.

"I got the address and time for the next client."

"Not about that. Just…" He breathed heavily into the receiver. "Just fuckin' get down here."

Click.

I barged into his office. "What now, asshole?"

He waved to a chair.

I sat and lit a cigarette. "Well? Need more broken teeth?"

"You been makin' a lot of fuckin' noise," he said. "You been fuckin' with the wrong kind of people."

"My problem."

"It's by my good graces, Rick, that you're not back in the fuckin' can."

"Good graces?" I asked. "You're a nothing. You're a fuckin' joke, Henry."

"The good news," he said, rubbing his cheek. "I made a deal to keep you out of danger. You'll work for me past your parole."

"No," I said, pulling out my gun, "I don't think so."

I unloaded all six rounds into his skull and drove off with adrenaline in my veins.

***

I went to Esmerelda's brothel.

"Rick?" a bouncer asked. "Haven't seen you in—"

Shot him and his partner and kicked in the door.

Driver

The bartender reached for a gun under the counter. Shot him.

"Esmerelda?" I yelled.

She ran to the bartender. "Why?"

Shot her in the eye, and spit on her corpse. "Bitch."

I left.

Chapter 35

I pulled up to the clinic and killed the engine.

"She's good, right?" Elizabeth closed her eyes, clutching the crucifix. "Please, Lord Jesus, let her be good."

Images of Maria banged around my skull. "Well, how many negroes make it through med school?"

Elizabeth rocked back and forth. "Hail Mary, Full of Grace, The Lord is with thee. Blessed art thou among women, and blessed is the fruit of thy womb, Jesus. Hail Mary—"

"The way I see it," I turned to face her. "You can enter the clinic, and a few hours later I'll drive you home, or in about fifteen minutes, a bus'll take you to a train station. Catch my drift?" I produced a crisp $100 bill. "Maria said to keep this for a rainy day."

Elizabeth waved it away. "I'm ok."

I insist.

"Ok," Elizabeth folded it and put it in her bra.

"Whatever choice you make, clinic or bus, I'll be here, understood?"

Elizabeth slammed the door and approached the driver's side. "Thank you."

"Ok, sure, off you go."

"No, really, you're the first person to care. I mean, really care." Her hands trembled and shivered as the wind roared. "You were a, well, I guess, the only person who ever listened, and in your own way, touched me with your heart."

I turned away. "Ok, no worries, off you go now."

"Thanks again, Rick."

Elizabeth began walking away and I slapped the dash. "Damn it, hold up."

"Why?"

"Most days I feel like a ghost, Elizabeth."

She closed her eyes. "I know."

I scribbled down numbers on a pad of paper. "This is an account number. Take it to any Wells Fargo branch, and you'll have around $7K. Maybe you could use this for, I dunno, a fresh start? New life? Become a world-famous mathematician."

"Rick," Elizabeth teared up. "I can't take this."

"Maria would want it." My hands shook as I lit my final cigarette. "For a guy pushin' 50? Doin' what I do? Ma time's pretty much passed. You need to take this."

"Rick, I—"

"Please." My eyes bled desperation. "You need to take this. Maria needs you to take this." I reached into my pocket and removed Maria's ring and kissed it. "This too."

"Rick, I…can't."

"Elizabeth, please. Take it."

"Ok." Elizabeth stuffed the paper and ring in her pocket. "Kindness is in short supply these days. I…well…I just—"

"Get goin' now. Bus'll be here in less than ten, and you're already late. But I'll be here." I took a long pause, and even longer drag, staring off into the night. "Yeah, I'll be here."

"Thank you, Rick." Tears rolled down her cheeks. "If I don't see you again, I hope you find peace someday."

About the Author

Sebastian Vice is the co-founder of Outcast Press and Translucent Eyes Press. His poetry and short fiction have made the rounds in the indie scene since 2021. His debut poetry book Homo Mortalis: Meditations on Memento Mori was published by Anxiety Press (2022).

Follow Sebastian on X @sebastian_vice

Also Featuring Sebastian Vice

An Anthology in aid of FIND - Helping Families in Need

Urban Pigs Press presents a collection of 23 stories by 23 different authors inspired by the prompt HUNGER. From gritty crime, realism, horror and everything in between. All profits will go directly to FIND - Families in Need to help tackle the global issue of hunger.

A collection of stories that are as close to the bone in literary class as they are in their scathing analysis of a broken society.
-Stephen J. Golds
Author of Say Goodbye When I'm Gone

Featuring the talents of Sophia Adamowicz, LG Thomson, Jacko Pook, Mathew Gostelow, Paige Johnson, Matthew McGuirk, Virginia Betts, Marek Z. Turner, David Cook, Neda Aria, Eddie Generous, Ann Hayton, Russell Thayer, James Jenkins, Bam Barrow, Sebastian Vice, Cassie Premo Steele, A.J. Stanton, Mark Burrow, Tabitha Bast, Rob Walton, Tom Leins and Jude Potts. Front cover by Jo Andrews (Mojo Art) and inlay by Cody Sexton (Anxiety Press). Foreword by Andrew Marsh of Dial Lane Books.

Part social commentary, part linguistic showcase, the authors of Hunger share such thought provoking stories of a feeling that no one is alienated from.
Some will leave you angry, some will leave you grateful and some will leave you with questions.
I would say it was a joy to read but more accurately, I am a more rounded person for reading it.
You're about to go on a journey. Where to? You will know when you get there.
- Rob Jelly

FIND

urbanpigspress.co.uk

Also Available From Urban Pigs Press

urbanpigspress.co.uk